"I think
pregna

Jordan felt herself blush beet red. She closed Ben's little black book hurriedly and handed it back. "I'm sorry," she said. "This is really none of my business."

"Oh, no," he insisted. "I'd like to have a woman's feedback. What do you think I should do?"

"Well, for a start, you could marry her," said Jordan, failing to notice the laughter in Ben's eyes.

"Oh, wow." He shook his head. "I don't think I'd want to go that far. I mean, Blondie's okay, but she's nothing special."

"Ben! How can you be so...unfeeling? I think you should call her, tell her you care...."

"I can't call right now." He frowned. "She's asleep."

Jordan glanced at her watch and said, "It's only nine o'clock. What time does she go to bed?"

"Let's see.... She usually goes to bed in, uh, January, and wakes up long about May."

Jordan stared at him, speechless.

Sarah Keene started writing when she was a child in North Florida's bayou country. "I would write plays, boss the other kids into acting them and stage performances before a patient audience of parents," she remembers. She credits the Brontë novels for making a permanent romantic impression on her. Sarah now lives in California, where she writes and works with children at the Los Angeles children's museum in her spare time.

Books by Sarah Keene

Don't miss any of our special offers. Write to us at the following address for information on our newest releases.

Harlequin Reader Service
901 Fuhrmann Blvd., P.O. Box 1397, Buffalo, NY 14240
Canadian address: P.O. Box 603,
Fort Erie, Ont. L2A 5X3

Earthly Treasures

Sarah Keene

Harlequin Books

TORONTO • NEW YORK • LONDON
AMSTERDAM • PARIS • SYDNEY • HAMBURG
STOCKHOLM • ATHENS • TOKYO • MILAN

ISBN 0-373-02828-8

Harlequin Romance first edition April 1987

CHAPTER ONE

THERE WAS NO DOUBT ABOUT IT, Jordan reflected as she sank into the soft bucket seat of the BMW and gazed at the profile of the man who was driving; Scott Townsend was a mover and a shaker. He was a natural-born salesman and he knew how to make things happen. In the three short months since their first date, he had courted her with a dedication that brooked no objection, and then before she quite knew what was happening, he had convinced her to marry him.

Jordan McKenna Townsend. She touched the engagement ring, an unfamiliar weight on the third finger of her left hand, and considered her imminent transformation. Last night they'd set the wedding date for the twenty-first of June.

June twenty-first! Two and a half months away! The thought sent a little chill down her back. She shivered in the cozy warmth of the small car and hoped that Scott had not seen. Scott—who never questioned himself or his decisions—made her feel somehow ashamed to admit that her own head was full of questions.

Come on, Jordan reasoned silently with herself. *You're twenty-five years old and you've always wanted a home and a family. And Scott . . .*

"Penny for your thoughts," he said now, reaching over to cover her fidgeting hand with his large one.

"You," she replied quietly. "Thinking 'bout you."

"Good!" He flashed the grin that had helped him become the fastest-rising young account executive at Weinstein, O'Connor and Associates, the advertising agency where both he and Jordan worked. It was generally agreed around the office that Scott Townsend had the stuff—the stuff of which company presidents are eventually made. He had ambition and know-how and it didn't hurt a bit that he also possessed a certain type of square-jawed preppy good looks. A fair-haired boy. One of America's favorite sons. Clients loved doing business with Scott. He could talk them into just about anything and make them enjoy shelling out thousands of dollars on a new campaign.

He had come into Jordan's life at a time when she was feeling especially low. Her father had died the preceding September after a brief illness and this, coupled with the loss of her mother a few years earlier, had left her with a terrible sense of emptiness at the center of things. She had felt homeless, adrift in the vast impersonal sea of Los Angeles, without family or even a long-time friend to provide some framework of support. True, there was an ancient aunt somewhere back east, and her sister, Hallie, lived in wedded bliss up in the remote wilderness of the Sierras, but there had been no one close at hand whom she could call late at night and to whom she could say, "I'm lonely."

Scott had changed all that. They had met when she had been assigned as copywriter to the Bicknell account, a project Scott was also associated with. He had taken an immediate liking to her work, not to mention her willowy blondness, and had suggested dinner at a fashionable new restaurant so exclusive it had neither a sign over the door nor a listed phone number. The customer had to know someone in order to get in. After her solitary, mournful diet of deli food and pizzas-to-go, Jordan was impressed.

They dined out together for the next seven nights in a row. As soon as she had gained a few welcome pounds, Scott insisted that she meet him at the gym every morning before work for a wake-up aerobics class. At first, she was so sore she could hardly walk, much less climb the stairs to her office, but by the following week, Jordan was beginning to feel pretty good. The look of melancholy was gone from her eye and her step had recovered its old buoyancy.

But Scott's plans for her renovation had only just begun. Soon he was advising her in everything—choosing her clothes for her, convincing her to use some of her savings as a down payment on a sporty new Fiat to replace her unsightly but comfortable old Rabbit, shopping for a few elegant additions to her apartment. "This is fun...but a little scary," she'd protested when she saw a beautiful Chinese rug stretched out on her living-room floor. "Scott, I don't know if I can afford all this. My credit cards are at their limit. I'm living way beyond my means."

"Nonsense." He had regarded her with an amused paternal air. "You're bound to be up for a promotion soon. And after we're married, our combined incomes should cover the expenses quite nicely. Just think, you'll come to me, a blushing bride, with all this as your dowry. And I'll be waiting there at the altar, willing to share my stereo equipment and my VCR and my personal computer with you for as long as we both shall live."

Jordan had had to laugh. "Is this a marriage?" she'd demanded. "Or a merger?"

"Both."

He was serious.

"Jordan!" Scott's voice boomed in the silence of the car, jolting her back into the present. "Is this it? The turnoff? Highway 180 going east?"

"Yes," she responded, sitting up and paying attention to the road. "Take the next exit."

They were on their way to the Sierra Forest Lodge, a small inn run by Jordan's sister and her husband high in the mountains near Sequoia National Park. Hallie and Petter Brundin were celebrating their tenth wedding anniversary with a party that evening and had invited the younger couple up for a weekend of cross-country skiing. A March snowstorm had covered the Sierras in several feet of powder. "It's fabulous. You have to come," Hallie had insisted to Jordan over the phone. "Besides, I want to meet that fellow of yours at least once before the wedding."

Scott had balked at the invitation and only after several days of pleading and cajoling on Jordan's part had he reluctantly agreed to go. "I've got an awful lot of paperwork to do," he claimed. "That stuff for Bob Bicknell. He's an important client and God knows I'd like to have him as a future ally."

"Scott . . ."

"I don't see how I can justify the time, sweetheart."

"Oh, Scott, it would mean so much to me to have you meet my sister and brother-in-law. They're the only family I've got and they're terrific people. Besides, we've never spent a whole weekend together, you and I, with no work and absolutely no mention of business."

It was true. Scott was, among other things, a die-hard workaholic. It made him nervous to be away from his office for longer than twenty-four hours. He was forever going in on a Saturday or a Sunday to put in an extra day's work.

Jordan hoped he would mellow—just a bit—with marriage. She, too, was good at what she did, but she was convinced that there was more to life than work and the nice things a paycheck could buy.

Once Jordan had teased Scott about being the ultimate yuppie, a young urban professional concerned first and foremost with getting ahead. He'd taken it as a compliment. "What else is there?" he'd asked. "Really?"

Jordan stared pensively out the window of the car as it began its gradual ascent from the flatlands outside Fresno up past orange orchards and small farms, over rolling hills and increasingly steep terrain toward the entrance of the park at sixty-five hundred feet. The landscape was aglow in the warm light of the late afternoon sun. Weary from four hours in the confinement of the automobile, Jordan stretched and yawned and in doing so, caught her ring in the weave of her sweater.

With this ring, I thee wed. She experienced a second faint shiver, like a drop of ice water trickling down her spine. Was she really ready for all this? Did she love Scott with that till-death-do-us-part sort of love? Well, she thought so. She certainly hoped so. But most of the time she was so impressed by him, so bowled over by his great confidence and verve that it was difficult to tell just what her deeper feelings were.

The coming weekend should help to clarify matters. They'd be together continuously over an extended period of time, not just meeting for aerobics or rushing off to some noisy dinner party. Surely she'd have a better sense of the man and her feelings for him after a couple of days in the peace and silence of the Sierra snows.

And of course she'd be seeing Hallie, frank, funny Hallie, her oldest confidant, who always knew how to cut straight to the heart of the matter. Hallie had the knack of being able to look at Jordan with her big brown eyes and put her in touch with what she'd been feeling all along.

Hallie and Pete were standing on the front steps of the lodge when Jordan and Scott arrived. "Hey!" The older woman's face lit up when she saw Jordan emerge from the car. "Mary Jordan! I thought you'd never get here!" The sisters rushed toward each other, slipping at the last moment on the icy path and falling into a comic embrace.

"It's a long drive." Jordan laughed as she tried unsuccessfully to recover her footing. "Oh, Hallie, it's so good to see you!"

"Well, you're just in time!" Hallie caught her sister's elbow and steadied her. "Dinner's in half an hour. Pascal has promised us something very special this evening. I don't know what it is; he won't let me in the kitchen! Now! Let's take your bags up to your room and..."

Scott had climbed out of the car and was busily introducing himself to Pete. Hallie glanced at him out of the corner of her eye and whispered to Jordan. "So far so good. Cute. Definitely cute."

"Scott!" Jordan called. "This is my sister. This is Hallie..."

He turned and gave Hallie his most charming smile, the one that Jordan had seen him use with important female clients. "Hallie," he began, "I've heard so much about you. And you're every bit as lovely as your sister. I can see the family resemblance."

"Aw shucks," Hallie drawled with a twinkle in her eye. "How you do talk, Mr. Townsend! This one—" she put her arm around Jordan's shoulder and gave her a squeeze "—this one's become so chic I hardly recognize her."

Studying the two women in the luminous twilight, an onlooker could in fact see many similarities and differences between them. They were both tall but Hallie was, by an inch or two, the taller of the two. She was lanky and angular and loose limbed whereas Jordan seemed somehow softer... and more contained. Each sister possessed a remarkable pair of dark brown eyes, widely set in an oval face. Hallie's looked directly ahead, inquisitive, sometimes even challenging. Jordan's, on the other hand, flitted and dreamed and then gazed out in utter openness.

With her ash-blond hair cut boyishly short, her face sunburned and devoid of makeup, Hallie was obviously most at home in her country inn. She favored jeans and plaid shirts and big sweaters, and whenever someone paid her a smooth-sounding compliment as Scott had done, she just shrugged and allowed her mouth to assume a humorous quirk.

Jordan's appearance reflected her big-city lifestyle—under Scott's careful tutelage. Her pale biscuit-colored hair fell straight and shining to a point about an inch above her shoulders in a simple yet flattering cut. Her mouth was fuller and more vulnerable than her sister's. And she wore her tasteful clothes—a soft angora sweater, a pair of wool slacks tucked into leather boots—with a quiet grace.

Upon first meeting Hallie, one felt that one knew her instantly. She was exactly what she seemed. Straightforward. No secrets. With Jordan, the effect was a good deal subtler. She was lovely, yes, possibly shy, but beneath the surface was . . . an undiscovered country. She was full of secrets, ripe with secrets, many of which she herself had yet to understand.

"We're pleased to have you, Scott!" Hallie announced in a cheery voice. "Come on. You must be freezing! Pete, grab that bag and let's get these folks inside."

A small suite of rooms had been prepared for Jordan and Scott. There was a cozy sitting area with a pull-out sofa and a rocking chair and a big picture window looking out over a range of mountains. Adjoining were the bedroom and a bath that, Pete assured them, featured an infinite amount of hot water, good for thawing toes and frozen fingers.

How clever of Hallie, Jordan thought when Pete and her sister had deposited the bags and gone. How clever of Hallie not to ask about the sleeping arrangements but to simply assign them quarters that allowed for all possibilities.

The truth was she and Scott had not yet consummated their relationship, and she had mixed feelings about it.

On one hand it had been a great relief to her that he had not pressured her, as had so many other men that she had dated briefly. Scott maintained a certain reserve; he enjoyed kissing her, of course, and holding her and he especially seemed to enjoy looking at her, as if she were a very special piece of sculpture he was helping to create.

But mostly they related on the level of personality. He liked to talk; he liked to discuss books and movies and the accounts he was working on; he loved playing mentor to Jordan and would spend hours explaining subjects she was unfamiliar with. And he seemed quite content to wait until they were married to initiate anything more intimate. At present his sexual energies were apparently sublimated into his work.

But . . . sometimes Jordan wondered whether or not he really wanted her. Perhaps there was something wrong with her, and that was why Scott was able to remain so cool.

Of course he must want her! she told herself for the umpteenth time. He was going to marry her, wasn't he?

Yes . . . but she wished that once, just once, he would forget himself and make a serious pass. She wasn't sure exactly how she'd respond, but she longed to see some reassuring spark of passion in his eye.

Maybe this weekend, in the beauty and the quiet of this place, something would happen.

DINNER WAS SERVED downstairs in the high-raftered dining room beside a glowing fireplace. The Sierra Forest Lodge cultivated a friendly family-type atmosphere; most of the guests knew it was their hosts' wedding anniversary and dropped by their table to wish them well. And, as Hallie had promised, the food was superb. Pascal, the gangling young Frenchman the Brundins had hired as cook that winter, had outdone himself, presenting them with roast duck in orange sauce and an array of tender vegetables. Even Scott, with his discriminating palate, looked content.

Six places had been set at the Brundins' table, Jordan noted. The fifth was occupied by Abby Goldman, a writer who rented the sole separate cabin on the lodge grounds. The sixth place directly to Jordan's left remained mysteriously empty. She wondered who the missing and obviously rude guest might be.

"What sort of writing do you do?" Jordan asked the plump affable writer across the vacant chair.

"I write for television," Abby told her. "I used to work for a soap but lately I've been doing night-time stuff. You know, hospital dramas, detective series, cops and robbers." She mentioned the names of a couple of popular shows. "I've been renting the cabin from Hallie and Pete for the past nine months. This is the only place I can seem to get any work done. There are too many distractions in Los Angeles."

"I know what you mean," Jordan agreed.

"So I drive down to the city whenever I have a story conference," Abby continued. "But mostly I stay up here and scribble. It's heaven."

Jordan was fascinated. "Do you—" Before she could shape her question, she was interrupted by the arrival of someone new.

"Ben!" Hallie's voice rang out in greeting. "You made it! Hurray!"

A gloved hand gripped the back of the vacant chair beside Jordan. She turned and found herself looking up into a pair of the blackest eyes she'd ever seen.

The man had just come in out of the snow. There were flecks of it on the shoulders of his jacket and sparkling white against the blackness of his hair. He had a most unusual face. Handsome and lean, something about the molding of his cheekbones made Jordan think that he must have Indian ancestry. But she wasn't sure. He could as easily have been French or Italian or a mixture of all three.

He was neither short nor tall, around five foot ten, she guessed, compact, graceful, with a sense of quiet but considerable power. His presence was most disturbing. Jordan felt the duck bob in her stomach and quickly looked away.

"Sorry I'm so late," he said, addressing Hallie and Pete. "A little trouble with Lily. But it's all right now."

"We're just glad you're here," Hallie assured him. "Introductions! Let's see. Abby, you know. And this is Scott Townsend. Scott, Ben Gerard."

The men exchanged hellos.

"And my sister," Hallie continued. "Mary Jordan McKenna."

Jordan winced at the sound of her full name. It had taken years to convince people to stop calling her

"Mary Jordan." With Hallie, the old habit still lingered.

Ben took off one glove and grasped Jordan's hand. The warmth of his touch sent an electric current racing along her arm and into her shoulder where it branched off in two different directions, reaching her heart and her brain at exactly the same time. For an instant, everything stopped. She felt paralyzed, short-circuited, like a city in a blackout.

"Mary." Ben Gerard gave her half a smile. "It's a pleasure."

"Jordan. Please," she heard herself respond defensively. "I prefer Jordan."

He laughed. There was a slight edge to his laughter that said he thought she was rather pretentious. He relinquished her hand, pulled out the chair and sat down. All around them, people had resumed their former conversations.

"Jordan, then," he agreed. His eyes swept over her, taking in the white angora sweater, the little silver earrings, the smooth line of her hair. "What's the matter?" he mocked. "Has 'Mary' gone out of vogue?"

"Not at all." She felt herself flush. "Jordan is my mother's maiden name. She had no brothers to carry it into the next generation so I thought I would."

"Ah." There was something unmistakably irreverent in his tone that made her want to punch him. Instead, quite without thinking, she reached forward and swatted the snow off the lock of hair that fell forward onto his brow.

Now Ben Gerard was the one caught off guard. He blinked in amazement as if he had thought her a proper little doll, incapable of spontaneous action. Raking his hand through the dampness of his hair, he broke into a wide grin.

"It's snowing again," he told her. His voice was casual but there was a new look of interest in his eye. "The skiing should be fine tomorrow."

"I hope so," Jordan responded, embarrassed with herself for having initiated this flirtation. "We've been looking forward to it."

"We?"

"Scott and I."

"Your boyfriend?"

"My fiancé."

His grin took on a satirical quirk. "Well, congratulations. Now that you mention it, I can see..." Ben glanced at her hand. "That's an impressive chunk of rock perched on your finger, ma'am. Hope you'll be very happy."

Jordan sat up a little taller and said in her most dignified voice, "I'm sure I will be."

Suddenly there was a flourish of music from the piano. Pascal was making his way toward the table, carrying a massive cake in both hands. As if on cue, the guests at the surrounding tables broke into a chorus of "Happy Anniversary to You." Hallie whooped and clapped her hands in delight and then leaned over to give her husband a noisy kiss.

When the cake had been deposited and admired, Pete Brundin stood up and invited everyone to partake. "Champagne and cake! Please, friends, join us!"

"Monsieur Townsend?" Pascal whispered. Jordan turned and saw the cook quietly handing Scott a note.

"A message for you. I believe they'd like you to call back right away."

Scott looked at the paper and frowned. "Thank you," he told Pascal before excusing himself from the table.

"What is it?" Jordan asked, laying her hand on the sleeve of his jacket as he was about to leave.

"I don't know. It's from my supervisor. I'll give him a ring and then I'll be right back." He patted her on the shoulder and was gone.

Time passed. Jordan finished her cake. She congratulated her sister and chatted with her brother-in-law and still Scott did not return. At Pete's urging, she accepted a second glass of champagne, although one was usually her limit. It was a special occasion, she reasoned giddily. But where was Scott? What was taking so long? She wished he were here, sharing in the festivities, getting to know Pete and Hallie, seeing how much fun a vacation away from L.A. could be.

Ben Gerard was deep in conversation with Abby Goldman, but suddenly, just for an instant, he glanced up and caught Jordan's eye. She felt once again that curious sensation underneath her breastbone, a pressure and a warmth. She was strangely affected by this man, and the realization made her angry. She stood up and turned to Hallie. "I'm going to the room," she said, "and see what's happened to Scott."

Hallie kissed her on the cheek. "Hurry back," she said. "This party's just begun!"

Scott was standing with his back to the door, putting the few items she'd unpacked earlier back into her suitcase.

"Oh hi, princess," he said when he heard her come into the room. "I'm glad you're here. I wanted to give you a little extra time to enjoy the party, but now I'm afraid we have to go."

Jordan was confused. "Go? Where?"

"Home." Scott closed the lid of the case and fastened the latch. "If we leave now, we can probably make it there by one."

Jordan rubbed her forehead. The champagne had made her feel a little goofy and she wasn't sure if Scott was playing a joke on her. "What are you talking about?"

"Steve Peretz is in the hospital with a slipped disc." Scott lifted the bag from its stand and deposited it by the door. "I believe I've got everything. Why don't you check the bathroom and be sure?"

"Scott! Just . . . just a minute. I'm very sorry about Steve Peretz, but what does his slipped disc have to do with us?"

"I'll explain it all to you in the car."

"No." She sat down uncertainly on the edge of the sofa. "I won't go anywhere until you tell me what's going on."

Scott gave her an impatient look. "My boss just called to say that Steve was out of commission and would I take over the Highgate account for him."

"Oh, Scott. Isn't there someone else who can do it?"

"Of course there's someone else who can do it! There are plenty of people who can do it!" He drummed his fingers restlessly against the leg of his slacks. "I'm just glad he asked me first."

"But what about . . . our weekend?"

"I've got a lot of catching up to do before Monday. Please, sweetheart, don't give me a hard time."

"Scott, you're overloaded as it is," Jordan reasoned, trying to control the dismay she felt. "You work sixty hours a week. Can't you take a break? Just once?"

"I like it this way."

"I only see you on the run. We're supposed to be getting married, and Scott...sometimes I feel scared, because I'm not really sure I know you! That's why this weekend was so important to me. I wanted us to spend some quiet time together. I wanted you to know my family." Jordan felt a knot tighten in her throat.

"We came for the party," he insisted. "I met everyone. You saw your sister. It hasn't been a dead loss. In fact, I'd say we've already accomplished just about everything that was necessary."

"We've been here less than three hours!"

"I'm afraid it can't be helped. I've already said yes to the account."

"Yes!" She felt her temper give way. "You said yes...just...like...that? You never talked to me or gave a thought to my feelings. Scott, it's not as if you need this particular job."

"It's an opportunity I don't want to pass up." Scott's eyes were steely blue now, like a lake frozen in winter. "Really Jordan, I expected you to be a little more supportive." He pulled on his coat and picked up their suitcases. "I'm taking these down to the car. Why don't you say goodbye to your sister and meet me in the parking lot?"

When she caught up with him a few minutes later, Scott was already warming up the engine. "What are you doing?'' he asked when she tapped on his window and motioned for him to lower it. ''Your door's unlocked. Hop in.''

''I'm not going,'' she told him. ''Give me back my bag.''

''Jordan!'' He was taken aback. ''What's the matter with you? I've never seen you behave this way before.''

''No,'' she replied with an odd laugh. ''I suppose you haven't.''

''Well, I can't say I like it.''

''That's because you only like it when we do things your way. Which is what we always do.''

''Just how do you suppose you'll get back to the city?''

''I don't know!'' She raised her arms in an expansive, reckless gesture. ''I'll have to work that out. But I'm not coming tonight. Scott, I need this weekend. I haven't seen my sister since the funeral, and I'm going to stay up here and visit. I'll get back on my own.''

The taut line of his mouth registered his disapproval. ''Have it your way,'' he said and flipped the switch that unlocked the trunk.

The moment she had taken out her bag and closed the trunk again, he put the car in gear and drove off, leaving her standing there, shivering in the dark. Impulsively Jordan scooped up a handful of snow, packed it into a ball and blindly threw it after the departing automobile.

There was a thud.

''Ow!'' exclaimed a husky voice. ''Who did that?''

Jordan gasped as a lone figure emerged from the blackness. In the light of the waxing moon, she recognized Ben Gerard, his hand pressed to his mouth, his eyes searching out the culprit.

"I'm sorry!" she cried. "Oh, I'm sorry! I didn't see you. Are you all right?"

He stopped just in front of her. "You!" he said, lowering his hand and staring at his fingers.

"You're bleeding!" Jordan winced. "Oh dear!"

"I think I split my lip." He ran his tongue across the inner edge. "Against my tooth."

"Oh Mr. Gerard, I'm so sorry..." she apologized again before bursting into tears. Suddenly all the emotion generated by her fight with Scott overtook her and she stood there in the middle of the parking lot, sobbing, her hands over her face.

"Hey," Ben said after a few minutes. "Lady. Come on, it's not that bad. I'll live."

"It's not..." Jordan tried to find her voice. "It's just..."

He became more sympathetic. "What are you doing out here without a coat?" Unbuttoning his own, he slid out of it and draped it over her quaking shoulders. "You'll catch a chill, city girl."

The coat was warm with his own body warmth and it had a musky, cedar smell. Jordan stopped crying and looked up at him.

Ben grinned and tapped her bag with the edge of his boot. "Running away from home?" he teased. "What's the matter? Have a fight with your boyfriend?"

"No! Yes! It's none of your business!" she huffed, furious all over again at the memory of what had transpired between herself and Scott. She was truly sorry she'd split Ben Gerard's lip, but she was in no mood to stand around in the cold and be interrogated. In fact she'd had quite enough of men for one evening. Jordan gave back the coat, picked up her bag and without further comment, marched off toward the lodge.

"Just a minute," Ben called after her. There was a note of consternation in his voice. "Slow down. I'll help you with that suitcase."

"I don't need any help!" she yelled. "I can take care of myself."

CHAPTER TWO

"I'M AFRAID I've done a rash thing!" Jordan confided to her sister over a mid-morning cup of tea. "Hallie, how am I going to get back to Los Angeles tomorrow? Is there a bus out of Fresno?"

Hallie picked up a poker and gave the logs in the fireplace a nudge. She stared into the flames for a long meditative moment and then her face brightened. "Abby," she said.

"Abby Goldman?"

"It's perfect. Abby has a meeting at Universal Studios first thing Monday morning. I'm sure she'll be glad to give you a ride into the city."

"Really! When do you think she'll be leaving?" Jordan asked eagerly.

"Tomorrow. She'll leave sometime tomorrow and stay overnight with a friend in L.A. You can ride down with her. She'll be happy to have the company."

"Oh! I'm so relieved!" Jordan lay back against the soft cushions of the sofa and extended her arms expansively across its back. The two women had taken advantage of the emptiness of the lodge at this hour— all the guests were off skiing—and appropriated the living room for their tête-à-tête. "Now I can enjoy my time with you! Hallie, you don't know how good it is to see you again."

"Well, you're always welcome here. I should have insisted that you come before, but I supposed you were busy with your job. I have thought about you, you know. I've thought about you a lot since Dad died—knowing you were alone, knowing I had Pete. At first I was worried. And then you met Scott . . ."

Jordan moaned. "Do you think I've blown it? Sending him back alone?"

"Pooh!" said Hallie. "I think the question should be the other way around. I think Scott Townsend should be asking himself if *he's* blown it."

Jordan looked at her sister in surprise. "I thought you were favorably impressed."

"I said he was cute. He is. But what if he's only beautiful on the outside?"

Jordan rose to the defense of her absent fiancé. "He has lots of good qualities. Really. You've seen him at a disadvantage."

"I think that's the best time to see people—at a disadvantage. That's when they show you what they're made of." Hallie paused and sipped her tea. "What do you think about the way you behaved last night? Tell the truth, Mary Jordan!"

Jordan sighed and hugged a pillow to her chest. "I don't know. I suppose I am feeling a bit guilty this morning. Maybe I'd had too much champagne. Maybe I wasn't understanding enough. Scott's career is awfully important to him."

"Amen to that," Hallie interjected wryly.

Jordan giggled. "Scott's career is awfully, terribly, horribly important to him! He doesn't work to live; he lives to work."

Hallie nodded.

"I'm not that way!" Jordan declared. "I enjoy my job, but I don't think it's the beginning and end of the world! In fact lately I've been thinking of switching to something else."

"Really?"

"Yeah. Maybe. But that's another story." Jordan brushed a wisp of hair out of her eyes as her face became serious once more. "We were talking about Scott. You know, Hallie, I have to admit I'm grateful to him. He helped me through the worst of a bad time. He got me moving and active and out in the world again at a time when I just wanted to retreat and hide. I don't know what I'd have done without him."

Reaching over, Hallie took her sister's hand in her own.

"But now that we've actually set a wedding date...I've got a case of the proverbial cold feet." Jordan's eyes shone as she studiously traced the pattern in the fabric of the pillow with the tip of her finger. "Sometimes I wonder if I've just been using Scott to fill up the empty place in me left when Dad died. Sometimes I wonder if I wasn't attracted to him because he was so ready to act like a father and to treat me like a little girl. When I'm with Scott, I don't have to make any decisions. He's happy to tell me what to do—what to buy, what to eat, who to be. Sometimes I feel like his child and sometimes I feel like his creation. And lately I don't know that I want to be either."

"Well, you're not a child," Hallie said gently, "and you're no one's creation but your own. You're your own woman and I think you'll start to feel better if you reclaim responsibility for yourself. I know it can be very tempting at times to give that responsibility over to someone else."

Jordan nodded. "You're right of course. Oh, Hallie, where do I go from here?"

"You have two choices. You'll either work things out with the man or you won't. But ultimately you'll do the thing that's best for you."

"You think so?"

"I'm sure of it."

Jordan made a wry face. "Well, I'm glad one of us is so certain."

"Mary Jordan, let me tell you something. I know how satisfying a good marriage can be, because I'm blessed in that particular area. But I'm not half a person just because I'm married to Pete. I'm a person and he's a person and together we make two. And I'm convinced that's the only way it really works."

"I envy you, do you know that?"

"Hey." Hallie's smile was warm. "Your time will come."

"Don't you and Pete ever get tired of being so perfect?" Jordan teased. "Doesn't all this...serenity get to be a little boring? Honestly, don't you wish you had some interesting problems—like mine?"

"Oh, it isn't going to be serene around here much longer."

"What do you mean?"

"Want to hear some terrific news?"

"Of course."

"I'm pregnant. Pete and I just found out for sure."

"No!"

Hallie laughed. "That's what I said at first. After all, we've been married for ten years. So much time has gone by that we'd just about given up hoping for a child. Then suddenly out of the blue—bingo!''

"Hallie!" Jordan rushed to embrace her sister. "That's fabulous! I'm so happy for you."

"You're about to become an aunt, my dear!"

"I can't wait!"

"Well, you'll have to. The baby isn't due until September."

"Hallie, now you've got to take special care of yourself," Jordan said, glad to fuss over her sister. "Hire someone to help with all the extra work around this place."

"Nonsense. I may not be a tadpole like you, but I'm only thirty, for heaven's sake. I'm in great shape. I intend to go right ahead with everything I'm currently doing."

"But don't you think you ought to at least take it a teeny bit easy?"

"No!" Hallie reached over and playfully tousled Jordan's hair. "You sound just like Mom used to! I'll take care of myself, but believe me, I have no intention of retiring into some kind of Victorian seclusion."

"Well, it's great news. I want you to keep me posted every week."

"Will do." Hallie hugged her again. "Come on, let's change into our ski clothes. As soon as he gets back, Pete has promised to take us over to Big Meadow."

THE DAY WAS SOMEWHAT OVERCAST, Ben Gerard noted as he parked his truck in back of the Sierra Forest Lodge. The sky was pewter colored with clouds, and he fancied that he and Pete might experience some snowfall on their trip to Big Meadow. He hoped so. He liked the hushed mystery of the woods at such times, and as long as there were only the two of them to be concerned about, they could go wherever they liked.

Besides Pete had promised to give him a few pointers on his technique. Ben was a good skier, but Pete had been a world-class professional in his native Sweden many years ago, before he'd married Hallie and emigrated to the States. A knee injury had forced Petter Brundin to give up downhill racing in favor of cross-country, and now he taught classes at the lodge and conducted the occasional trek.

"Halloo! Ben!" Ben heard his friend call out from the forest of skis and poles stuck upright in the snow beside the lodge. "The ladies are joining us! They've got their gear on and we're ready to push off."

Ben was surprised to see Hallie waving merrily in his direction. Well, so much for his idea of exploring new trails alone with Pete. Hallie would want to take a tamer route. Still she was a practiced skier and a good sport. He liked her. She was fun-loving and she rarely complained and she shared his enthusiasm for the countryside.

But there, standing next to her in a silver-blue suit so new and fashionable it might have been cut from the pages of a magazine, was the temperamental younger sister. Jordan. He groaned and touched his lip. She'd walloped him in the face with a snowball the previous night and then inexplicably stormed off when he'd tried to help her out.

No doubt her stuffy fiancé was somewhere close behind.

For a moment, he considered begging off. A pair of greenhorns like those two were bound to slow things up. But the fact was he needed the exercise. He'd been sitting at his desk in his house at Ash Mountain all morning buried under a mound of reports, and he'd been looking forward to the fresh air and the physical thrill of skiing through the frosty woods.

"Ben! What a nice surprise!" Hallie greeted him when he'd unloaded his equipment and hiked over to join them. "You remember my sister?"

"Sure. Miz McKenna." He acknowledged Jordan with a cool nod.

"Mr. Gerard." The girl didn't seem any more pleased to see him than he was to see her.

"Actually he's Dr. Gerard," Hallie teased, "even though he'd have us all believe that he's just some lonesome cowboy who wandered down from the high country."

Jordan seemed surprised. "You're a doctor?" she repeated.

"Not a medical doctor," he informed her as he knelt to fasten his skis. "I'm a research scientist. I work for the park."

"Ben has a degree from Berkeley in bear-ology," Hallie volunteered. "He's up here studying the bears. He's a wildlife expert."

"So to speak."

"He is! He is!" Hallie enthused. "He's been asked to write a book about our black bears, but he just won't sit down and do it."

"I like the field work," he protested, "not the paperwork. I'd much rather spend the day with an animal than a typewriter."

"Come on, you snailpokes!" Pete prompted, poised and ready at the base of the trail. "We haven't got all day."

Hallie glanced at her husband and giggled. "Slowpokes!" she corrected. "The word is slowpokes, Pete."

"Yah...slowpokes. That's right," he conceded. Even after twelve years in America there were some words that continued to mystify Pete. With an easy, gliding motion, he moved off now, his long strong legs breaking trail for the rest of them through the newfallen snow. Hallie slipped her hands into the straps of her poles and swiftly followed his lead.

Ben looked around in search of the stuffy fiancé. "Anybody else coming?" he asked Jordan.

"I'm afraid not," she replied, avoiding his eyes.

Apparently she and her friend had had a serious squabble. Perhaps the fellow had even gone off and left her stranded. Ben remembered a car speeding into the dark seconds before he'd encountered Jordan's snowball.

He touched his lip again. Well, it was really none of his business. He'd come to ski, not to catch up on the latest gossip. Deciding for safety's sake to bring up the rear, he motioned her onto the path, and in a moment they were off.

The view from the trail was breathtaking, despite the overcast sky. In the distance the mountains were a pale and luminous blue, and to the west, one could see the magnificent panorama of peaks and plains stretching toward the Pacific. Ben drank in the cool clean mountain air and felt his head open. It was a giddy sensation, more intoxicating than fine wine. He was an ardent lover of the wilderness, and just the thought of spending the next few hours sailing through the cedar forests on light-weight skis was enough to restore his good spirits.

By the time Jordan stopped to take a snapshot, he was feeling downright sociable. He pulled in beside her and planted his poles in the snow. "It's something, isn't it?" he commented, noticing the rapt expression on her face.

"Hmm," she sighed. "It certainly restoreth my soul."

"Is your soul in need of restoration, Miz McKenna?"

"Maybe," she agreed, gracing him with a smile. For a skinny little city slicker, the girl was not bad-looking, Ben decided. He had studied her briefly the night before but had eventually dismissed her as not being his type. Too haughty. Too uptight. And otherwise engaged.

But now, breathless and rosy-cheeked from the exercise, she had a whole new appeal. There was something fresh—and decidedly sexy—about her.

"When you live in a city," she was saying as she fiddled with the light meter on the camera, "you rarely see the horizon, not like this anyway. There's always another building a few feet in front of you, blocking out the sky."

"Lost Angeles." He laughed and made a face. "How anyone can live in that polluted wasteland is beyond me."

He'd meant it as a joke but he could see from her expression she hadn't taken it as such. "Unfortunately," she began, the haughtiness now back in her voice, "not all of us can afford to be purists like yourself, Dr. Gerard! Some of us have jobs in the city. Some of us have homes and friends and a whole life there."

He shrugged. "I suppose it all depends on what you value most," he said gruffly. What a prickly thing she was! Ben glanced at the trail in search of Hallie and Pete. "C'mon," he advised, "let's go. We'll lose sight of the others if we stay here much longer."

"You go ahead." Jordan waved him on. "I've skied this trail before with Hallie. Just last year in fact. I know the way."

"Uh-uh." He shook his head. "I think we should all stay together in twos and fours. Look at those clouds. It could start to snow at any moment and then where would you be?"

"I'll be fine," she insisted stubbornly. "I want to wait until the sun comes out so I can take this picture."

"You may be waiting all day."

"Oh please! Go ahead. I'll catch up with the rest of you in a few minutes."

Now Ben was concerned, and more than a little provoked. He'd suspected from the beginning that she would somehow complicate the trip. But what could he do if she was bound and determined to be pigheaded? "Well," he growled, "if you get lost, don't expect us to send a St. Bernard after you."

"Goodbye, Dr. Gerard," she said coolly as she turned her attention to the view through the lens of her camera.

With a snort of displeasure, Ben pushed himself back onto the trail and set out in search of more amiable company.

Out of the corner of her eye, Jordan watched him depart on his skis, graceful as a dancer. In a moment, he had rounded the curve, his crimson jacket and dark head disappearing into the grove of fir trees. She sighed. The man was more attractive than she cared to admit, and she was disturbed by the pull he exerted on her. But she didn't have time to get to know Ben Gerard just now. She was much too preoccupied with worrying about what she was going to say to Scott Townsend.

In the distance a lone hawk hung in the frosty air, riding the currents. Jordan wished for an instant that she were that bird, free and solitary, without all the concerns that currently crowded her thoughts. She raised the camera and tried to get a reading on the light meter. Ben had been right about one thing. The sun was never going to come out. She snapped the picture anyway and hoped for the best.

When she returned at last to the trail, Jordan realized that the others had gained quite a lead. Well, no matter, she knew the way...or at least she thought she did. The massive trees loomed on either side like silent sentinels in the frozen landscape. Strangely, she couldn't remember exactly how far she'd come or how much farther she had yet to go before she reached the fork in the trail where a signpost pointed the way to Big Meadow and toward the smaller Rabbit Meadow.

And to make matters worse, a light snow was beginning to fall. Jordan squinted. If she tried, she could still make out the trail markers, blue badges nailed to the trunks of the trees. Oh, it was going to be all right. It had to be. She'd assured Ben she knew the way and she didn't want to wind up looking like a dope. Not in front of Dr. Know-It-All.

Fortunately she was in fairly good physical shape. All those aerobic classes Scott had relentlessly dragged her to had increased her stamina as well as the strength in her legs. She was able to handle the incline with ease and in just a little while, she had reached the fork in the trail.

Now where was that sign? She glanced around. It was nowhere in sight, probably buried underneath the snowdrift. The question was, was Big Meadow to the left or the right?

Jordan hesitated. The trail had been broken in both directions and she didn't know which set of tracks to follow. *The left,* prompted a voice in her head. *It must be the left.*

Thirty minutes later, it was apparent that she had made a mistake. The trees opened out and she recognized the long narrow expanse of Rabbit Meadow. Her heart sank. The snow was falling heavily. Reaching into her pocket, Jordan pulled out a fuzzy cap and put it on, tugging it down around her ears.

Darn. Darn. Darn. There was nothing to do but turn around and head back the way she'd come. The others had surely missed her by now. Hallie and Pete were probably worried and Ben Gerard was no doubt gloating that his assessment of her had been correct all along. She was just an ignoramus who barely knew her left ski from her right.

Above her head an ancient cedar groaned. Jordan looked up just in time to see an avalanche of snow descending from its overladen branches. As she ducked and threw up her arms to protect herself, she lost her balance and went careening down the hillside. Arms flailing, powerless to stop, she fell and rolled and tumbled and fell some more until she landed face first in the white sea of the meadow.

At first she was content to lie there. Then, when she gradually ascertained she had lost neither life nor limb, Jordan gingerly raised herself to her elbows and wiped the snow from her mouth.

"Hey," cried a voice from the hillside. "Are you okay?"

Through the veil of falling snow, Jordan recognized a crimson jacket. Ben. The last person she cared to have rescue her! She'd rather freeze to death than hear him say, "I told you so."

But he was traversing the hillside, making his way toward her. Jordan braced her poles against the snow and tried to raise herself to her feet, but just as Ben arrived, she lost her balance again and down she went.

"Are you all right?" he demanded, gliding to a stop. He had a scowl on his face as if he were personally upset with her.

"Perfectly," Jordan responded.

"Sure you didn't break anything?"

"I'm fine!" she insisted, hot with embarrassment.

"Need a hand?" He extended his.

"No thanks."

He stood there, watching with an intensity that made her nervous as once more she struggled to her feet. Succeeding this time, Jordan planted her poles to one side, brushed off the snow, and then, with a look of triumph, she reached again for the poles. And fell.

Now she heard him chuckle, a low noise muffled in his throat as he tried valiantly to maintain a stern face. "Don't you dare laugh!" she threatened, shaking her fist, feeling bruised and powerless and at the end of her reserves.

"I'm sorry," he apologized. "I'm sorry. But for such a refined creature, you're quite the best pratfall artist I've ever seen."

"Well, I'm not exactly doing this for your entertainment!"

"I know. Please, take my hand and let's get out of here before they have to send a search party for both of us."

Jordan sighed. "Where are Hallie and Pete?"

"I told them to go back to the lodge. There's a big party arriving from San Francisco at five and they had to be there to greet them." Ben took off his glove and brushed the snow from his eyelashes. "I had a hunch what had happened to you and I assured them I'd bring you back alive."

"Hmm," Jordan observed wryly, "aren't I lucky?"

"Yes ma'am, you are. Now cut the sarcasm and give me your hand."

She hesitated.

"Look," he said, his patience abruptly gone. "I said I'd bring you back and that's what I'm going to do—even if I have to tie a rope to you and drag you.

Now you can choose, Miz McKenna, which way you prefer to travel.''

Reluctantly she took his hand. Ben hoisted her to her feet, but their skis had become entangled and this time they both fell. Ben landed on his back and Jordan felt her head strike his chest.

"Good grief!" he rasped, his voice hoarse as if he'd just knocked the wind out of himself. "This is getting to be ridiculous!"

She raised her head and found herself looking directly into his eyes. They were so fiercely black and said he thought she was far more trouble than she was worth. At the same time, she noticed the swelling on his lower lip where she had hit him with the snowball. He had a beautiful mouth.

For a moment, Ben stared back at her and then, amazingly, he began to laugh. "We're hopeless," he announced. "Hopeless!" The sound was infectious and before she knew it, she was laughing too. For a moment they remained exactly where they were, on their backs in the snow, helpless with hilarity, both struck by the absurdity of the situation.

"C'mon," he said, sitting up at last. "One more try! Let's go!"

THE WARMTH OF THE FIRE felt fabulous. Jordan stood with her back to it, toasting herself with a blissful expression on her face. "Well," Ben told her approvingly, "you're starting to look like a real live girl."

She raised her eyebrows questioningly. "What did I look like before?"

"Oh, I don't know." He settled back into his chair and propped his boots up on the stone rim of the hearth. "When people first come up here from the city, they always seem a little harried. As if they've got a bunch of wheels inside their heads, all turning ninety miles an hour. They're preoccupied. They're either living in the future or the past but certainly not in the present. Then, after a couple of days in the mountains, they calm down and the real person begins to shine through."

Jordan considered this for a moment. "I guess I have been pretty cranky," she admitted. "I'm sorry. Most of it had nothing to do with you."

"I didn't think so," he said.

"Thanks for the help this afternoon. I do appreciate it."

"You're welcome."

"Are you staying to dinner?"

"Am I invited?"

Jordan smiled. "I'm sure Hallie and Pete will be happy to have you. If it wasn't for you, I'd probably be lying frozen to death under the snow in Rabbit Meadow."

"I doubt it," he replied, wincing at the image. "But I'll stay anyway."

"Good. I'll go tell Hallie and see you in the dining room."

Hallie approved at once of the idea. "Of course he should stay! But dinner's going to be about ten minutes late," she said, fretting over lamb chops in the kitchen. "Pascal and I are running behind. Why don't you run upstairs and change out of those damp clothes? You've got time."

On her way to her room, Jordan stopped by the reservation desk to check for messages. It had been almost twenty-four hours since Scott had driven off without her, and she wondered if perhaps he'd called.

"No ma'am," the clerk told her. "Nothing for McKenna."

She frowned. He was still angry, Jordan thought as she took the stairs two at a time. As soon as she reached the room, she picked up the phone and dialed the number of Scott's apartment. His answering machine informed her he was not home. She hung up and tried the office.

"Yeah. Townsend. What is it?" said an impatient voice on the other end.

"Scott. It's me. Jordan."

"Jordan. Where are you?"

"At the lodge." She took a deep breath. "How're you doing? Still mad?"

"No...no..." He sounded distracted. "I'm busy. What's up?"

"Well, I just thought I'd let you know I've found a ride home."

"Fine. See you Monday."

"Scott..."

"What?" There was the sound of rustling papers and a desk drawer being opened and shut. "What is it? Jordan, I can't talk."

"Don't you have anything...to say to me?"

"Have a good time. Have a ball. I've got to go. I'm really swamped here."

"Right," she said. "Bye."

There was a click on the other end.

For a moment, Jordan sat motionless on the edge of the bed, still holding the receiver in her hand. He hadn't even said goodbye. He couldn't spare an extra

second to say goodbye, much less "I'm sorry" or
"how are you?" or "I love you." It was obvious
where she came on his list of priorities. Right down at
the bottom.

Peeling off her ski clothes, Jordan climbed into a
hot shower and allowed the pulsating water to mas-
sage the taut muscles in her back and neck. She and
Scott had a lot to work out as soon as she got back. If
this marriage were ever to take place, they had to come
to a completely new understanding. It was essential.

In the meantime, she might as well take him at his
word and have as good a time as possible. Emerging
from the shower, she quickly dried and changed into
a pair of cocoa-colored slacks and a soft pink cowl-
necked sweater. *Yes, have a good time,* she told the
face in the mirror, *have a ball!*

AFTER DINNER, she turned to Ben Gerard and said, "I
don't think I care for coffee. What I'd really like is an
Irish coffee in the bar. Can I buy you one?"

He gave her one of his quietly piercing looks that
made her feel as if he could see right through to the
back of her brain. "No ma'am," he said. "But you
can buy me a Scotch."

She was flirting with the man, she knew, but somehow she just couldn't help herself. It was fun. And
buying him a drink made her feel a little macho. After all, Scott had told her to have a good time. And
since Scott's concern for her was zilch at present, it
was reassuring to know that someone enjoyed her
company.

They adjourned to the cozy little bar and found a
table by a window that looked out over the moon-

swept snow-covered landscape. Ben took off his jacket and draped it over the back of his chair. As he did so, a small black notebook fell out of his pocket and landed, open, at Jordan's feet. She picked it up.

"Dr. Gerard," she teased. "You've dropped your little black book."

"Thanks," he said, reaching for it. "Where would I be without my little black book?"

"Not so fast." Jordan playfully refused to relinquish it. She took a sip of her Irish coffee and casually looked at the opened page. "Oh my gosh!" she exclaimed. "It really is a little black book. Look at this! 'Lily.' And then a bunch of dates and numbers." She scanned the page and then looked up at him with renewed curiosity. "Lily... I heard you mention her last night. She'd been causing you some trouble...."

"Lily," Ben said, "causes a lot of trouble. But she's worth it."

"Is she?" Jordan felt a twinge of disappointment. Of course a man as attractive as Ben Gerard must have had a girlfriend. It was inevitable. She took another sip of her drink. Well, what was it to her? she asked herself. This was just a silly little flirtation they were having. It wasn't going anywhere.

"Alicia, on the other hand," Ben continued, "causes much more trouble than Lily and I'm afraid I may have to write her off."

Wide-eyed, Jordan stared at him. She turned the page and sure enough there was the name "Alicia" written in block letters at the top. So the man had not one but two girlfriends. Interesting. "Dr. Gerard, you do get around!" she murmured.

"I do." His eyes were dancing. "It's true. I do."

Jordan turned another page. "'Blondie'..." she read incredulously. "Blondie? Sounds like a singer in a rock band. What's Blondie's story?"

Reaching across the table, Ben took her hand in his and said in a confidential tone, "Jordan, can you keep a secret?"

She nodded. "Of course."

"I think Blondie may be pregnant," he whispered.

She felt herself flush beet red. Jordan closed the book hurriedly and handed it back to him. "I'm sorry," she said. "This is really none of my business."

"Oh, no," he insisted. "I'm glad to have someone to talk it over with. It's been on my mind a lot lately and I'd like to have a woman's feedback."

Jordan looked at her drink and then at the floor and then she looked at Ben again. "What do you intend to do about Blondie?" she asked.

He shrugged. "What can I do?"

"Well, for a start, you could marry her."

"Oh, wow." He shook his head. "I don't think I'd want to go that far."

"Ben!" Jordan took back her hand.

"I mean, Blondie's okay but she's nothing special."

"How can you be so... unfeeling?"

"What would my other ladies think?" He seemed genuinely perplexed. "I can't take myself out of circulation. Jordan, listen, I can't tell you how much those girls look forward to seeing me—"

"Excuse me," Jordan interrupted. "Excuse me but I think I need some fresh air. The amount of ego in this room is making it a little hard to breathe." She started to stand up but he caught her by the wrist.

"Please," he said, "don't go. Not yet. I'm really interested in what you have to say."

Rather than cause a scene, Jordan reluctantly resumed her seat.

"So," Ben began in a more contrite tone, "you think I owe Blondie something?"

"I think you should go to the phone and call her immediately. Let her know you're there. It's terrible to be cut off and ignored by someone you care about."

He nodded, apparently giving her suggestion his full consideration. "I can't call right now." He frowned. "She's asleep."

Jordan glanced at her watch. "It's only nine o'clock," she told him with a look of disbelief. "What time does she go to bed?"

Knitting his brows, Ben thought for a long moment. "Let's see... she usually goes to bed in... January, and she wakes up... long about May."

"What on earth are you talking about?"

"Blondie's a bear, Jordan." He could scarcely contain his mirth. "Lily and Alicia and Blondie, they're a bunch of bears. And I'm very fond of them all."

Jordan stared at him. For a moment she could not think of a single response. He'd been putting her on! And she had fallen for it, hook, line and sinker. Despite herself, she began to laugh.

"Come on," Ben said, grinning, obviously very pleased with the success of his joke. He finished his drink and put his empty glass down on the table. "You wanted some fresh air. Let's go for a walk. It's stopped snowing.''

"You . . . !"

"Yes?"

"How could you do that to me?" She hiccuped between convulsive fits of giggles. A tear appeared in the corner of her eye and rolled helplessly down her cheek.

"You really set yourself up for that one." He chuckled. "You did! Rummaging through my notebook!"

"Yes, but—"

"Yes but nothing. Besides, I just wanted to hear you laugh. You need to laugh more, Jordan."

"I do laugh," she countered. "I laugh plenty. This afternoon—"

"No. I think you laugh now and then. But mostly you worry."

The man was disturbingly perceptive. Just now, with her sides aching and her vision a little blurred, she felt better than she'd felt all weekend. "Let's walk to the pond," she said, taking him up on his suggestion, "and see if anyone is ice-skating."

He cocked an eyebrow. "Sure you won't be cold?"

"Well, I'm not going to worry about it!" she retorted. "Heaven forbid I should worry about anything."

The night was ablaze with stars, each one sharp and dazzling clear above the shaggy tops of the surrounding cedars and fir trees. In the hushed silence, there was only the sound of their footsteps, boots crunching against the snow, as they wound their way down the path toward the pond.

"Is Blondie really pregnant?" Jordan asked, smiling again at the very thought of the ruse he'd perpetrated. And with such a straight face!

"It's more than likely," Ben agreed. "We'll see. She may have a couple of cubs with her when she emerges from her den."

"How do you keep track of her?"

"She's wearing a collar equipped with a radio device around her neck. We outfitted her with it last year. Blondie's quite a feisty old girl and she wasn't easy to capture." He shoved his hands into his pockets. "Oh look," he said as they came in view of the pond. "There's no one here. Too bad."

Jordan wandered over to a sheltered bench and sat down. The empty pond glinted like a dark mirror in the moonlight.

"Do you skate?" Ben asked, stopping behind her and placing one foot on the bench. Jordan turned sideways to look at him. She was struck again by something Indian in his features, which was especially apparent when his face was in repose. Her gaze followed the strong line of his cheekbone, taking in the dark hollow below it, his firm chin, the chiseled outline of his mouth.

"Do you?" he repeated.

She shivered. "What?"

"You're cold! I knew it!" He unzipped his jacket.

"No, no." Jordan shook her head. "Don't give me your coat, Ben. I'm fine. Really," she said and shivered again.

He straddled the bench, sitting down and pulling her against him with her back against his chest, wrapping her in the warmth of his open jacket, closing them both inside. "I was asking if you like to skate," he reiterated. She could feel his warm breath ruffling the top of her hair.

"I . . ." She could hardly think for a moment. His nearness had such a startling effect. Jordan could almost hear her own heartbeat pounding in her ears. "I, uh, haven't skated . . . since I was a child," she managed. "I've forgotten how, I suppose."

"No," he disagreed. "One never forgets . . ." And then quietly he began to whistle, a solitary, piercing sound in the quiet of the night. The melody was familiar, though she couldn't place it. A waltz? Something to which she had danced or skated long ago. . . .

The minutes passed. Jordan felt her whole being grow warm and expansive; she was melting into Ben, wrapped so snugly next to him in the cocoon of his jacket. A thick, sweet, dreamy sensation flooded her limbs. She probably shouldn't be here, she thought. She really ought to go. But she found she had no desire to leave.

At last he released her, taking her hands in his own and giving them a brisk, final rub. "Better?" he inquired. "Warmer now?"

She gazed at him, half-hypnotized. Noticing again the small swollen place on his lower lip where she had walloped him with the snowball, Jordan extended her fingers and touched it very delicately. "Your mouth," she murmured. "Does it hurt?"

"No," he said quietly.

She ran her fingertip over the place and looked into his eyes. *What are you doing!* a small voice whispered inside of her, but she could not bring herself to heed it, so great was the spell under which she had fallen.

He caught her hand. "Jordan..." he began, frowning. "Don't. I'm not the one you want. Come on, let's go. This is crazy."

Her eyes brightened as a terrible need arose within her. A need to touch and to be touched. Ben sucked in his breath. She saw a curious mixture of pain and desire in his face. Then in one swift movement, he caught her head between his hands and his mouth came down on hers in a rough, hungry kiss. She gasped, arched toward him and suddenly his tongue was in her mouth, a dark, tantalizing sensation.

With a cry, she pulled away, frightened by the strength of her own response.

"Jordan..." Ben reached for her but she eluded him. Blindly she rose from the bench and stumbled backward. "Jordan, wait," he said.

She could only shake her head. "Don't look at me," she whispered.

Uttering an oath of frustration, he stood, walked to the edge of the pond and then came back again. She could see his breath, short puffs of white visible in the night air. "Not exactly what you bargained for," he decided. "Somehow I didn't think so. What you really want, Miz McKenna, is a little revenge on that fiancé of yours. Just a little. Not too much." He laughed. "Well, fine, you've got it."

Flustered and humiliated, she could think of no response. Turning on her heel, Jordan fled up the path toward the brightly lit safety of the inn. She knew he was watching her, though he made no attempt to follow. She could feel his gaze burning into her back.

It was true. She'd flirted shamelessly. She'd tempted him. But she'd never meant for things to go so far.

Or had she? an inner voice nagged.

CHAPTER THREE

JORDAN HAD BARELY OPENED her eyes when an acute sense of embarrassment prompted her to pull the covers over her head and hide. The morning sunlight flooding the lodge bedroom brought back the reality of the place and the memory of what had occurred the previous night. Ben Gerard! She'd practically thrown herself at the man! She, Mary Jordan McKenna, perennial nice girl and the fiancée of another man, had been so overcome by a momentary attraction to a stranger that she'd actually...

In a flush of recall, she experienced again the ferocity of his kiss and the longing it had awakened within her. And the kiss was nothing compared to the dream she'd had later, much later, when she'd at last been able to fall asleep.

Throwing off the covers, Jordan leaped out of bed and made a beeline for the shower. As Pete had promised, there was a seemingly endless supply of hot water and she was able to stand for a full twenty minutes with it pounding down upon her until her fingertips shriveled and the air was dense with steam.

Frowning, Jordan stared for a long moment at the soapy diamond ring on her left hand and thought of Scott. Although they might be having difficulties at present, she was engaged to the man and that was a commitment. At any rate, this crazy, dangerous flirtation with Ben Gerard was not the answer to her problems. If anything, it was a form of escape, a way of avoiding responsibility. She had to put it out of mind.

Jordan turned off the water with a decisive twist of the knob. Drying and dressing hurriedly, she noticed with a glance at the travel clock that it was almost ten a.m. Goodness, she'd been so distracted the previous night that she'd forgotten to set the alarm. Well, Hallie would just have to take pity on her and give her something in the kitchen. Abby Goldman wanted to leave before noon and there wouldn't be time for lunch.

Downstairs in the empty kitchen, she found a pot of coffee still warm on the stove and the remains of a coffee cake, which had not yet been put away. Hungrily, Jordan helped herself. Just as she had taken a big mushy raisin-filled bite, she heard the door swing open behind her and turned to see who was there.

It was Ben.

The cake flew down her windpipe and in a moment she was choking helplessly. Tears shot to her eyes and she covered her face with one hand while the other groped blindly for support against the kitchen counter. To her humiliation, the sensation refused to pass and she continued to cough for a full two minutes.

At last, Ben came to her aid. With one arm, he caught her across the shoulders while his other hand vigorously patted her back. "Oh!" she moaned when she could speak at last. "I am so embarrassed!"

He turned her around to face him. "Well, don't be," he said levelly. "It happens to everybody. Sooner or later something goes down the wrong way."

Jordan reluctantly raised her eyes to meet his. He seemed handsomer than ever, fresh and clean smelling with his chin newly shaven. The bruise from the snowball had almost entirely disappeared, and in looking at his mouth, she remembered the thrilling havoc it could wreak.

"It's not just this," she told him, swallowing hard. "Ben, I'm embarrassed about last night. I owe you an apology."

"You do?"

"What must you think of me behaving the way I did?"

A ghost of a smile danced across his lips. "You were something," he agreed. "You were a real vamp for about five seconds—until I took you up on it."

Jordan blushed. "What must you think of me?" she repeated, shaking her head.

"Oh..." He reflected for a moment and then spoke. "I think you're a little mixed up right now. You're having some trouble with your boyfriend and so you're ricocheting around here, not quite knowing what to do with yourself."

"It's true," she admitted. "I behaved like an idiot. I'm sorry."

"Hey, would you stop apologizing and offer me a cup of coffee? There's no harm done. It was just a bad idea...on both our parts. I'm certainly willing to forget it if you are."

It seemed to Jordan that he was over his displeasure of the previous evening and was taking the whole thing in his stride—as if women made fools of themselves around him all the time. Which they probably did. Flustered, she searched through the cabinets for a clean cup. "Do you take cream? Sugar?" she asked, finding a cup and filling it.

"Black, please. Pete and I are driving into Fresno to pick up some supplies and I need a pick-me-up." He rubbed his eyes. "I've been at work since dawn, monitoring a couple of bears over the radio."

"And how is Blondie?" she asked, happy that he had changed the subject.

"Sleeping like a log."

"And Lily and Alicia?"

"Staying out of trouble—at least for the time being."

Jordan placed the steaming cup on the counter in front of him. "Tell me, Ben," she began, willing herself to sound as casual as he, "how'd you ever get into this line of work?"

"Do you really want to know?"

"Yes!"

"Well, it's kind of a long story. Basically, I think it comes down to destiny."

"Destiny?" She cocked her head to one side, instantly curious.

"Yes, ma'am, destiny," he said with a grin. "When I was growing up, I used to spend the summers with my grandmother who lived, oh, a ways north of here in the mountains. Her Christian name was Eliza Stone, but actually she was a Shoshone Indian and her real name was Singing Bear. Most everything I've learned that's worth anything came from her."

"What? Tell me."

"It's not that easy to put into words." He sipped the coffee and thought for a moment. "The knowledge I received from my grandmother came more from just being with her than from anything she said. It had to do with the reverence she had for the earth and all the creatures that inhabit it. This may sound corny, but somehow she impressed upon me that the animals were my brothers and that my destiny was linked with theirs."

Jordan was fascinated. "Go on," she urged.

"Well, Grandmother passed away when I was about twelve. But later, when I was going to university in Berkeley, I had an idea that I wanted to do something in the area of ecology and wildlife preservation. And eventually I hooked up with a professor who recommended me for a field project in Yosemite National Park. I earned my degree by spending three years studying the bears in Yosemite."

"What fun! Did you live in a tent in the woods?"

"No." Ben smiled. "I lived in a house with my wife."

Jordan looked up, startled. "I didn't know you were married."

"I was."

"Past tense."

"Past tense," he confirmed. His face was quiet and composed, but Jordan thought she saw a flash of pain in his eyes.

"What happened?" The question popped out before she had time to consider its appropriateness.

"She was killed in a hiking accident. She fell and broke her neck."

"Oh!" Jordan instantly regretted having pressed him. "How tragic. I'm so sorry."

"Yes. It was . . . very sad."

"I'm sorry I brought it up."

He took a few moments to finish his coffee and then he spoke again. "It's been almost four years. I don't mind talking."

Jordan watched as he delicately replaced the china cup in its saucer. He had rough woodsman's hands. The nail on the thumb was blue where he'd apparently banged it. But there was such sensitivity in his small movement that she found herself touched. Suddenly she felt close to him, as if they had developed a new intimacy. "What was her name?" she asked.

"Mary."

"Mary," Jordan repeated. "My first name is Mary, too."

"That's right," he said. "The name you don't use."

"What was your Mary like?"

"She was . . . terrific. What can I tell you?"

"Anything you like."

"Mary Elizabeth Hanauer and I went through college together. We married the day after graduation. We were just a couple of babies. We were certain we knew everything there was to know and that we'd live forever." His tone was rueful, his voice even. Beneath it, Jordan sensed an enormous reservoir of feeling held in check. "She was a generous, independent-minded, outspoken woman and I was crazy about her."

"What did she look like?"

"Tall. Athletic. Brown hair. Blue eyes. And an overbite."

"An overbite?"

"Yeah. I've always been partial to overbites. I think they're sexy." He smiled. His eyes were very sad. "At any rate, we had three good years together before she died. And I'm thankful for that."

"Three years..." Jordan echoed. She didn't know how people survived such things. "It hardly seems fair."

He shrugged philosophically. "Who says life is fair?"

"Well..."

"Life is fragile, precarious, an ever-changing proposition—at least that's what I think. Sometimes it's sweet and sometimes bitter. There's no point trying to hang on to the sweetness because it will pass. And there's no point dwelling unnecessarily on the bitter because, well, it's not much fun."

Jordan looked at him for a moment. "So what do you do now, Ben Gerard?" she asked.

"I stay very loose."

The kitchen door swung open and Hallie entered the room, interrupting their conversation. "Ben, there you are," she said. "Pete's out back loading some crates into the truck and he wants to know if you can lend a hand."

"Sure thing." He plucked a raisin from the coffee cake and popped it into his mouth. "I'm off. Thanks for the coffee, Jordan."

"You're welcome," she murmured.

"Whoops," Hallie commented when he had gone. "Did I barge in at the wrong moment? You have a most peculiar look on your face, Mary Jordan."

"No, no...we were just talking. Ben was telling me about his wife."

"Oh. Yes. Mary Gerard. That was a very sad affair."

"Did you know her?"

Hallie shook her head. "We first met Ben when he transferred from Yosemite to Sequoia National Park shortly after Mary died."

"Well, he seems to have come to terms with it—at least in his own mind."

"So he'd have us believe."

"You don't think so?"

"Well—" Hallie had found a tin box and was busily putting away the remains of the coffee cake "—he's in a hundred-times-better shape than he was when we first met him, that's for sure. But whether or not he's made his peace...I don't know. I think he keeps himself a bit aloof."

"Surely he's not a hermit."

"No. He's too attractive for that. But it's my impression that he's much more interested in those smelly old bears than in any of the women I've seen him with."

"Yes," Jordan said and then fell silent. Slowly she picked up their empty coffee cups and rinsed them in the sink. What a contradictory creature he was, she thought. On the surface, he had a humorous charm. But underneath, he was very intense. Suddenly she recalled the startling urgency of his kiss the night before. There had been hunger in that kiss, and longing, and a kind of passion she'd never experienced before. He was lonely, she realized. For all his seeming to be in control, Ben Gerard was a lonely man.

"Sweetie," Hallie was calling her back from her reverie, "would you do me a favor? Run out to the parking lot and take this thermos of tea to Pete before he drives off. You've got your boots on and I don't, and I'd rather not step outside."

"Will do." Jordan accepted the thermos and slipped quickly out the back door.

Ben was sitting behind the wheel of the pickup truck, warming the motor, which hiccuped loudly in protestation of the cold, when Jordan knocked on the window. "A present," she called, waving a tall silver thermos, "to Pete from Hallie." Opening the door, he took it from her and placed it on the seat. "Pete'll be along soon," he said. "I'll make sure he gets it."

"Well..." She wavered for a moment, wobbling on the ice in her boots as if she wasn't sure whether to stay or go. He watched, charmed by her coltishness, until she had become thoroughly self-conscious. "Bye," she said at last. Raising her hand in a farewell gesture, Jordan turned to leave.

"Wait a minute." He stopped her with his voice.

She dug her heel into the snow and slowly pivoted to face him.

"Come here."

She took a couple of steps toward the truck.

"When are you leaving?" he asked, reaching for her hand. It appeared as small and as smooth as a child's between his two weathered ones. The flow of electricity was instantaneous.

"In about an hour," she replied. "Abby's giving me a ride to Los Angeles."

"Ah. You're leaving today. Good."

Jordan raised one eyebrow. "What do you mean, good?" she asked in mock indignation.

"I think it's good that you're going home. Patch things up with your fellow. Get married." He kissed the back of her hand cavalier fashion.

Jordan stared at him, a fresh rush of color darkening her cheeks. "Thanks for the good wishes, Dr. Gerard," she retorted sassily. "I'm glad I have your personal blessing."

"When I see you again, you'll be Mrs.— What's his name?"

"Townsend."

"Townsend," he repeated. "Well, so long Jordan. And all the best."

As she turned to go, she heard him lean back against the creaky springs of the front seat and utter a long deep sigh that sounded very much like relief.

To Jordan's surprise, Scott seemed eager to make amends. A large bouquet of roses was waiting for her at her apartment when she arrived home Sunday evening. The card that accompanied the flowers read: "Dinner after work tomorrow? Missed you."

True to his word, he whisked her off to an early supper at Spago, a fashionable restaurant, as soon as they had finished at the office. He was even willing to listen when Jordan, mustering her courage, determinedly outlined what she felt to be the problems in their relationship.

"Fine," he said when she had finished. "I'm really glad you brought it up, princess. Things are going to be much better from here on out. You'll see."

Jordan stared at him in amazement. She had expected some resistance, a few arguments at least, but not this glib agreement. For a moment she wondered if Scott was smooth-talking her, promising her everything without really thinking twice.

He smiled, perfect white teeth in a winsome face. "You want to make your own decisions? I'm all for it. You can always count on me for support, Jordan."

"Great," she murmured.

"And I'm going to make sure we have more time together in the future. In fact, I'll make it a priority."

"Wonderful." What else could she say? Perhaps he really meant it. Perhaps there was some chance they might work out their differences after all.

"I hear you're going to be writing the new magazine ads for Adonis," he said, changing the subject. "That's terrific, Jordan. If you do well on this one, you'll be up for a promotion in no time."

"I can't really think about the promotion." She sighed. "All I can think about is the campaign. One step at a time, please. This one is a toughie!"

"Well, do think about the promotion!" he advised. "If you get one, it'll do wonders for our combined annual income. We'll be able to put a down payment on that condo."

"Why the rush? I thought we were going to live in your apartment for a while. It's plenty big, Scott, and I like it."

"No," he disagreed. "It's big enough for the two of us, but we're going to want to do some serious entertaining after we're married. So we'll need something roomier and a lot more impressive."

"I'm just a little reluctant to spend the money from a promotion before I've even been awarded one."

"Don't worry." He leaned over and gave her a kiss on the cheek. "You'll get that promotion. I picked you for a winner the first day we met."

ADONIS WAS THE NAME chosen for a new cologne for men to be launched by Bicknell Enterprises, a company heretofore responsible for a successful line of skin-care products. Jordan had worked for Bob Bicknell before and had disliked the experience. Not content with being president of his own company, Mr. Bicknell fancied himself an authority on copywriting as well, which drove Jordan crazy. After hundreds of hours spent coming up with just the right concept, just the right headline, she would submit her copy only to have the man rewrite it to suit himself. And in her opinion, his revisions were always for the worse.

Sure enough, when she finished her first draft of the new Adonis ads, Bicknell objected to almost everything. He objected in particular to the use of the words *cologne*, *scent* and *fragrance*. "Too sissy," he decided. "This is a product for real men, not a bunch of sissies, and we don't want to use any sissy words."

"Do you think *scent* is a sissy word?" she asked Scott, who as account executive was responsible for relaying Bicknell's opinions to her.

"It doesn't matter what I think," Scott responded. "Bicknell thinks it's a sissy word and that's all that counts."

"But we've got to tell the customer what it is he's buying," Jordan insisted. "At the moment there's nothing in the ad to tell him whether it's a cologne or a skin bracer or a bottle of nitroglycerin. We can't just leave people in the dark.''

"You're a smart girl. You'll think of something.''

Grumbling, she picked up a small bottle on the corner of her desk, uncorked it and offered Scott a whiff. "Have you smelled this? It's awful. I wouldn't like Adonis if it was given away by the barrel.''

"Jordan, your job is to sell Adonis to the public. It doesn't matter whether or not you like it personally.''

"I know.'' Jordan rubbed her temples with the tips of her fingers. She'd had a headache ever since she'd come home from the mountains. "But sometimes it gets to me, you know.''

"What gets to you?''

"Well, it's all so absurd. Here I am promising the American man that if he wears Adonis, then presto, his whole life will improve. Women will fall all over him. He'll be rich and successful and sought after. If he puts on a single drop of Adonis, he'll turn into James Bond!''

"So?''

"So it's a lie!'' Jordan laughed wearily. "I'm sitting in my office lying to people every day.''

"You're just tired. Hey, I've heard about a great new French-Chinese restaurant. Why don't we go there tonight?''

"I just wish I was doing something I believed in, Scott. I wish the whole thing weren't so meaningless.''

"Jordan!'' His voice took on an authoritative tone. "I don't want to hear any more of this kind of talk. It's counterproductive. You have a very good future with Weinstein, O'Connor and Associates and I won't let you talk yourself out of it. Do you hear? Now get back to work.''

Jordan got back to work. She racked her brain and produced a completely new draft for Bicknell's approval. But the dissatisfaction she had expressed to Scott continued to grow and fester in her mind. Copywriting had been fun in the beginning... especially when she was promoting a product she had genuine enthusiasm for, but now, with each month that passed, it seemed to become more and more torturous. Perhaps she was in the wrong business! Perhaps she was of the wrong temperament for a career in advertising. Perhaps there was another line of work she was better suited to.

Jordan turned the matter over in her head every night before she fell asleep. Something deep inside her rebelled against the work, and she feared that if she continued, she might soon develop writer's block and not be able to produce at all.

And to complicate matters, she continued to have reservations about her rapidly approaching marriage to Scott. Despite his promise to spend more time together, he was still down at the office working through every weekend. And when she talked to him, he put on an attentive face and nodded and made a show of listening, but she always had the feeling that his mind was somewhere else.

Late at night, before sleep finally claimed her, Jordan had an image of herself rushing pell-mell into the future—a future with a man she rarely saw, a future in a job that wasn't right for her. And just before she was swallowed up into the blackness of it all, she saw Ben Gerard's face smiling a gently mocking smile.

"I QUIT," she told Scott as he finished the last bite of the dinner she had prepared in her apartment. She'd labored most of the afternoon, fixing his favorite dishes, hoping that the good food would put him in a receptive mood.

He gave her a quizzical look. "You quit what? Aerobics? Jogging? What, princess?"

"I quit my job. I turned in the final piece for the Adonis campaign and then I walked into Mr. Weinstein's office and I quit."

Scott put down his fork and stared at her wordlessly.

"I know I've done the right thing," Jordan was quick to assure him. "Copywriting may be the right career for any number of people but, Scott, it's just not right for me."

"Are you out of your mind?" he whispered.

"No." She shook her head. "No, I'm not." Oh dear, she'd begun this all wrong. She hadn't meant to blurt it out. Jordan had known he'd be upset but she hoped she could persuade him to see her point of view.

"Jordan, I thought we were getting married next month!" Scott pushed his chair away from the table and rose to his feet in disbelief.

"Sweetheart, you're not listening. I've only quit my job. I haven't abandoned you."

"Well, how do you suppose we're going to manage?"

"I've some money in the bank," she offered. "Between that and what you make, we should be able to get along. At least until I can find something else."

"And when do you think that will be?"

"I'm not sure. I need a little time to work this all out. It's an important transition for me." She reached for his hand. "Please. Sit down. I've made dessert. We can have a cup of coffee and talk this through."

He ignored her invitation. "Jordan, I think you're being incredibly naive. You were up for a promotion at Weinstein, O'Connor and Associates."

"Maybe. We don't know that."

"I've already worked out a budget for the coming year based on our combined annual income."

"Oh?"

"There's just no way we can go ahead with some of our plans if you quit your job."

"But it's already done. Mr. Weinstein accepted my resignation."

"Then you must go back tomorrow and apologize and ask him to reconsider."

"No," she insisted quietly. "I won't. Scott, we may not be able to afford a new condo and a cellar full of champagne right at first, but we can get along very well. You know we can. Besides I fully intend to go back to work."

He paced the room as he loosened his tie in frustration. "You're being completely irresponsible," he accused. "Just because you're feeling bored, just because you've had a little trouble with one account is no reason to—"

"I am being responsible!" Jordan interrupted, trying to keep a rein on her emotions. "Really. I've given it a lot of thought. I need to find out who I am, and what it is I do best—"

"That's a lot of nonsense! For heaven's sake, what did you do, Jordan? Read some article by some nutty psychiatrist in some nutty magazine? What's this sudden need to find yourself?" His voice was full of scorn. "Everything was going just fine!"

"Was it?"

"Jordan, I believe that you have a lot of potential. And I've devoted a considerable amount of time to helping you develop it. You're bright and you're attractive and you're well liked at the office. And to quit your job now, just when you're on the verge of becoming—"

"Someone I don't want to be?" She finished the sentence for him. "Scott, you have helped me and I appreciate it. But I'm the only one who knows what's right for me! I can't live my life as your protégée! I think you'd get pretty bored with me if I did. Remember when you said I could count on you for support? Well, this is when I need it."

"How can I be supportive when I see you throwing away your future hand over fist? I don't have time for this, Jordan. We don't have time for this. We're adults, both of us, and it's a little late for you to be ditzing around trying to decide what you want to be when you grow up."

Jordan felt something inside of her snap. "If this is so impossible for you," she flared, "then maybe we'd better postpone the marriage." The words sounded hollow and tinny as if someone else had said them. For a moment she and Scott stared at one another. He looked oddly like a stranger. There was nothing familiar in his face with which she could connect and feel comforted.

"Yes." He nodded. "Maybe we'd better."

Jordan was shocked. She hadn't expected him to agree so readily. "Scott," she began, her voice shaky, "why did you ask me to marry you to begin with? Was it only because my salary was a nice addition to yours?

Was it because you thought I'd make a good hostess at your parties?''

"I asked you, Jordan, because believe it or not, I care for you. And I think we can build a good life together.''

She shook her head. "Perhaps what you mean by a good life and what I mean by it are two different things entirely.''

"You're just upset.''

"You're darned right I'm upset!'' She worked the diamond ring off her finger and held it out to him. "Here. Perhaps you can find another princess with a better dowry.''

Scott refused to take it. "Uh-uh,'' he said. "I'm not giving you up. If you're bound and determined to take the time off, if you feel you need to find yourself, then go ahead! We'll postpone the damn wedding!''

"Scott—''

"Then after a few months—in the fall perhaps—we can sit down like two rational adults and begin to plan a future for ourselves.''

Jordan took his hand and uncurling the fingers, she pressed the ring inside. "I don't feel comfortable wearing this.''

"Jordan! I'm only considering this a temporary—''

She fought back the tears. "Oh Scott, I'm afraid it's just never going to work out!''

CHAPTER FOUR

WHEN SCOTT HAD GONE, Jordan picked up the phone and called her sister. "Wow!" Hallie exclaimed when Jordan had poured out the whole emotional story. "Good for you, Mary Jordan. I'm glad you stood up for yourself. How did you two finally leave things?"

"Oh..." Jordan rubbed her forehead wearily. "He's sure I'll come round to his way of thinking sooner or later."

"Natch."

"He hopes that in a few months I'll come to my senses, that I'll settle down and be a good little yuppie wife."

"So as far as Scott's concerned, you're still engaged."

"I returned the ring. Hallie, the way I feel just now, I don't see how we'll ever get back together."

"Hmm." Hallie made sympathetic noises. "What do you plan to do with all this new freedom?"

"Who knows?"

"Why don't you come up here?"

"What?"

"You could have a bit of a vacation, clear the smog out of your head, write the Great American Novel."

Jordan laughed. "No thanks! I don't think I want to write another word as long as I live."

"Now, Mary Jordan—"

"I mean it. I'm burned out. That last project for Bicknell really did it. I'd like to take my typewriter and drop it off the end of the Santa Monica Pier."

"Careful...careful..."

"I'd rather do something physical...with my hands instead of my brain. Do you need a cook? Or a gardener? How 'bout a woodchopper?"

"As a matter of fact—"

"Great! I'll take the job! When do I start?"

"I know you're joking, Mary Jordan, but the truth is..." Hallie's voice held a new note of seriousness. "I need you. Do you think there's any real chance that you could come?"

"Why? Is something wrong?" To the best of Jordan's knowledge, Hallie had never before asked for help. She felt a ripple of disquiet.

"I wasn't going to mention it, 'cause I knew you were busy with wedding plans and all the work at the office, but now..."

"Don't keep me in suspense! Is something wrong at the inn? Did Pascal leave you and go back to France?"

"No, no, it's me."

"What about you?"

"I saw the doctor this week, and he seems to think I'm going to have a 'difficult' pregnancy. I'm supposed to stay off my feet. I'll be in bed for the rest of the summer."

Jordan was instantly concerned. "Oh, Hallie," she murmured, "you gonna be all right?"

"Well, it's a big adjustment," Hallie moaned, then laughed in the same breath. "You know me. I'm a very active person. If I had my druthers, I'd be hiking and swimming and running around right up until the actual birth.''

"I'm sure you would.''

"Dr. Simon says no way. That's the bad news. However, if I follow his orders—stay home and do absolutely nothing—we'll both come through this okay, me and the baby.''

"How can I help?''

"Take over for me. Hostessing here at the inn. Overseeing things. Pete's got his hands full already. We have a small staff of course, but there really needs to be two people in charge.''

"How soon do you need me?''

"Right away. Oh, Mary Jordan, can you really do it? Without sacrificing your own life?''

"My life? My life is in chaos! There's nothing to sacrifice.''

"I mean, as long as you're between jobs...''

"I'd be glad to help. You're my sister. I love you. Besides, it'll be a good break for me. A chance to get my head together and decide where I go from here.''

"Thanks a million! You don't know what a relief this is! It'll be so nice for me to have you close by.''

"I'll come upstairs and read to you every afternoon—from Dickens—while you lie among your pillows.''

"Forget Dickens. Come up and play poker. I'm going to be stir crazy!''

Jordan glanced at the calendar on the wall in front of her. "I'll need at least a week to square things away. Can you hold out till then?''

"Just knowing you're on your way will make all the difference.''

"Hallie, I'll see you soon."

Six days later, Jordan could scarcely believe what she'd accomplished. First, she'd found a friend of a friend who was eager to sublet her apartment for the duration of the summer, thus relieving Jordan of the extra burden of the rent. Next, she'd packed up several hundred dollars' worth of unused merchandise that Scott had persuaded her to buy and returned it to the stores. Finally, she'd thrown a few clothes and books into two suitcases and tossed them into the car.

Feeling as free and bewildered as a fledgling bird, she flew the coop of the city and winged her way once more toward the Sierras.

Pete met her in the lobby of the inn. "Florence Nightingown!" he said. "Are we glad to see you!"

"Nighting*ale*." Jordan gave him a big hug. "Hi, Pete. How is she?"

"Taking a nap. Let's get you settled first and then you can go upstairs and say hello."

"Fine. Which room is mine?"

"We thought we'd put you out in Abby's cabin. That way you'll have a bit of privacy."

Jordan was surprised. "Where's Abby?" she asked.

"Gone to New York. She got some TV job—writing for a new show. She'll be away for at least six months."

"And she won't mind? My moving in?"

"Nooo." Pete sang the word in his Swedish lilt. "She'll be happy to have someone staying out there keeping an eye on things. She was afraid a squirrel might come in under the rafters and make a nest in her books."

Jordan laughed.

"Here, give me that bag." He reached for the larger of her two suitcases. "Off we go! Watch for the puddles!"

A light rain had fallen earlier that morning, and the woods surrounding the lodge were now ghostly with mist. Pete and Jordan picked their way along the soggy path, each carrying a bag and holding the other arm outstretched for balance.

"Yuck!" she protested. "You were right. I just got a shoeful of mud."

"High heels!" Pete regarded her with an amused look. "You won't need them up here. I hope you brought galoshes."

"They're in the bag you're carrying." Jordan sensed the moisture seeping down into the toes of her favorite Italian pumps. Well, she'd wanted a change of pace, and apparently she'd got it. No more dressy dinner parties. No more supper at Spago.

"The snows have been melting for the last month," Pete informed her, "but soon the sun will come out full-time and then there'll be more wildflowers than you've ever seen in your life. Here's the cabin!"

Nestled in a clump of trees a couple of hundred yards from the main lodge, Abby's little cabin looked like something out of the Brothers Grimm. The A-frame structure was built of rough-hewn cedar, gently weathered by the passage of time. Depositing the suitcase on the porch, Pete inserted a key in the lock and opened the front door.

"Oh!" Jordan sighed as she wiped her shoes on the mat and stepped inside. "It's wonderful." The cabin was basically one open space divided into two levels; living room, kitchen and loft bedroom all shared a common ceiling. The walls were natural wood and Abby had upholstered the furniture in peachy spring-time colors. If one looked, one could see the evidence of Abby's profession: shelves of books, a desk laden with paper and an orange mug overflowing with pencils.

"Abby has a typewriter, too," Pete commented, "but Ben borrowed it last week when his own went on the blink. We'll have to petition him to get it back. You may want to use it."

"Uh-uh!" Jordan was adamant. "I'm not even going to write a letter."

"Sure. If you say so." Pete's easy-going tone said he would not press her about career matters. "I'll tell him to keep it then."

"How is Ben?" she asked, her curiosity piqued. In the chaos of moving, she'd scarcely given a thought to the enigmatic Dr. Gerard. "What's he up to?"

"The bears are just starting to emerge from their dens." Pete opened a window, letting some fresh air into the stuffy room. "So he's out in the woods playing scientist. We haven't seen him much."

"Oh."

"Let's see. Do you have everything you need? Any other suitcases in the car?"

"Just a few groceries."

"You didn't have to do that."

"I brought Hallie some fresh fruit from the Chalet Gourmet. Don't worry though. I'll put on my galoshes and fetch it myself. It's only one small bag."

"Then I'll run along. Give you a chance to unpack. Come over when you're done and we'll all have supper in Hallie's room."

"Thanks, Pete."

Hallie was overjoyed to see her. The two hugged and wept and gossiped throughout the dinner Pascal prepared. "I'm so glad you're here," Hallie told her over and over again. "It's going to be a wonderful summer after all!" For her part, Jordan was relieved to see that her sister looked healthy and seemed as spirited as ever, despite her condition.

Later when she was alone, curled up on the sofa in front of the cabin's hearth with an afghan and a newspaper, Jordan found her mind wandering back over the events of the past week. How quickly things had turned around! All of their lives were in transition. Her own, of course. Hallie's and Pete's with the coming baby. Even the earth was bursting into new life after the long white silence of winter. Ben Gerard's precious bears were waking up and lumbering forth from their dens in search of adventure. Jordan yawned and snuggled down into the depths of the afghan. The heat from the fire was making her drowsy and in a few minutes, she had drifted into a dream where all thoughts merged in a kaleidoscopic whirl.

IF HE SQUINTED, Ben could just make out the faint glow of light at the end of the path. Good! That meant Abby was still up. He'd intended to return the typewriter earlier that afternoon, but he'd had to stop off at the ranger station in Grant Grove to pick up a report. One thing after another had arisen to detain him and now it was most decidedly late.

Shouldering the typewriter, he sloshed his way through the puddles dotting the trail, careful not to trip and drop the confounded thing. He knew Abby was leaving for New York any day now and he thought she might want to take it along. It was her "lucky typewriter," the one she'd carried around since college, and she'd loaned it to him only after extracting a solemn promise that he'd protect it with his life.

When she failed to respond to his knock, Ben was puzzled for a moment. The lights were on, the chimney smoking. Well, perhaps she was over at the lodge, having a nightcap with Pete. He fished under a flowerpot, found the spare key and inserted it in the lock.

The door creaked open.

Stepping into the room, he quickly glanced about. Everything was silent, save for the crackling of a log on the hearth. It wasn't like Abby to go off and leave a fire untended! For safety's sake he decided to check it out. Leaving his muddy galoshes at the door, he crossed the floor in his stockinged feet.

And then he saw the girl.

She was lying on the sofa, sound asleep, with her arm over her head. A colorful afghan had worked its way off her body and was now tangled around her feet. She was slim and blond and wore some sort of peignoir, a fancy silken thing—quite an exotic item in this neck of the woods where everyone favored flannel pajamas or long underwear or both on a particularly cold evening. He wondered who she was.

As if in answer, she turned in her sleep, gravitating toward the warmth of the fire and revealing her face. Jordan McKenna! Good heavens but she was lovely! Especially now in repose, all defenses down, that clever, fretful mind of hers turned off for the night.

He remembered Jordan McKenna very well. He'd been attracted to her and frustrated by her and relieved to see her depart. That had been months ago. So what the devil was she doing back again, and ensconced so sensuously in Abby's couch?

He could tell by the faint movement behind her eyelids that she was deep in a dream. A happy one, or so it appeared. A little smile danced across her lips and her breath was soft and even, giving gentle swell to the soft curves beneath the lace.

Ben felt an ache pass through him. *Time to go, Gerard,* he told himself with a touch of rue. Kneeling, he swiftly adjusted the screen in front of the hearth. There was nothing much left of the fire. It would die out soon and then she'd wake up cold. Lifting the edge of the afghan, he pulled it up to cover her.

At the touch of his hand, Jordan's eyes flew open. For a quarter of a second she gazed at him in wordless wonder. And then she screamed.

"Jordan!" he said. "Jordan, hush!"

Clutching the afghan to her, she scrambled to her knees and screamed again.

"Jordan, it's me. Ben Gerard. It's all right! Sorry I frightened you..."

She glanced around the room, drowsy, disoriented, as if she didn't quite know where she was. "What are you doing here?" she asked in a hoarse voice.

"I brought back Abby's typewriter. I—"

"Abby left for New York two days ago."

"Already? Damn. I hope she didn't need it."

Jordan rubbed her eyes. "I'm sure there are typewriters in New York," she drawled with a trace of the old haughtiness. But she was still half-asleep and couldn't quite pull it off. Ben had to smile.

"I guess there are," he agreed.

She gave him a dirty look. "You scared me half to death! I was dreaming. I was sound asleep and dreaming."

"I know. You were in REM."

"What?"

"Rapid eye movement. That's how you can tell if a human, or an animal, is dreaming."

She considered this for a moment and then she frowned. "How long have you been standing there?"

"About a minute. Maybe two."

"Well, I'm not some bear, you know! I'm not here for observation. It's none of your business if I dream or REM or—"

"Relax, Jordan. I didn't mean to invade your boudoir." He bit off the word, satirizing her concern. "I just wanted to make sure you didn't burn the place down."

"How did you get in anyway?"

"Hey, are you always this cranky when you wake up?"

"What's it to you?"

"Absolutely nothing."

The flatness of his answer took her by surprise. Ben watched for a moment as she warily descended her high horse and became a little more cordial. "Sorry." She raked one manicured hand through the sheaf of pale hair that had escaped from her ponytail and fallen forward into her eyes. "I've just had a long day, driving up from the city, and I guess I conked out after dinner. You really did spook me!"

"I know. Strange man in your house and all that."

"Not so strange," she admitted. "Hello, Ben."

"Miz McKenna." He nodded. "What brings you back to this part of the country?"

"Oh—" Jordan wrapped the silken robe around herself and belted it at the waist "—I'm here for the summer... helping Hallie out until the baby comes."

"Mighty generous. Thought you had some high-powered job down in L.A."

"Not anymore. I quit."

Now it was his turn to be surprised. She'd struck him as a real *Yuppie americanus*. Female of the species. Career-oriented. Luxury-loving. He watched as she daintily suppressed a yawn with one hand. And then he realized she was not wearing the ring. "What happened to the rock?" he asked.

"What rock?"

"The last time I saw you, you were wearing a diamond big enough to feed Ethiopia."

She regarded him with renewed exasperation. "I gave it back."

"How come?"

"Is that any of your concern?"

"Maybe. Maybe not."

"You are such a snob! It wasn't that big of a diamond! It was just an ordinary, average, medium-sized diamond. I'm not as superficial as you imply, Dr. Gerard."

"Did you really break up with old whatsisname?"

Jordan placed both hands on her hips. "You know what you are?" she asked.

"No. Tell me."

"Nosy!"

He shrugged. "To a scientist like myself, that's a compliment. Yes, ma'am, we're always nosing around asking lots of questions. We like to know all the whys and wherefores.''

''Well, it's late. And I'm not willing to discuss it. So why don't you just wander over to the lodge and check on the nocturnal habits of your friend, Br'er Pete? I believe he's still tending bar.''

''Jordan—''

''Scott and I split up! All right? Now go away, please, and leave me alone. I'd like to get some sleep.''

Apparently the break was still fresh. Ben noted her flushed cheeks, the staccato movements of her hands as she turned away from him, seized a scrap of newspaper, crumpled it and thrust it into the fire.

For his part, he didn't know whether he was pleased or dismayed by her news. He'd already dismissed Jordan McKenna as an available woman. He'd married her off in his mind long ago. And attractive as he found her, there was something in him that preferred to keep her once removed.

But he was attracted to her! That was the problem. He didn't want to be. He recognized the potential for involvement and he just didn't want to explore it. If he had any sense, he'd take her at her word—get out of there and leave well enough alone.

Only... just not... Looking at her in the firelight, he wasn't sure he wanted to have any sense.

JORDAN WATCHED as the paper ball ignited and burst into blue flame. She was provoked with Ben—with his holier-than-thou witticisms, with his presumptuous questions that probed into areas she had yet to resolve for herself. Yet at the same time she couldn't help remembering the way he'd once kissed her, down by the pond on a snowy winter's evening.

In her haste to leave Los Angeles and make herself available to Hallie, she hadn't really thought much about seeing him again. Oh, she'd figured he'd show up sooner or later. But she hadn't counted on to-night.

And she hadn't counted on the current between them remaining quite so unflaggingly intense.

The room was hushed. She glanced his way. He was still standing there in his stockinged feet looking at her, his eyes as fierce and dark as she'd remembered.

"Jordan," he began, "I'm sorry if—"

Suddenly the air was pierced by a loud noise. Only a hundred yards or so from the cabin, it sounded as if something were being ripped to pieces. There was a shattering of glass and the heavy crunch of metal.

Ben was instantly in motion. He raced to the door, tugged on his boots, and pulling a flashlight from his pocket, he threw open the latch and disappeared into the blackness.

"Ben!" Jordan called, running out onto the porch. "Be careful!" The fog swirled heavily about the cabin, chilling her to the bone. Another crash indicated that somewhere nearby a door was being torn from its hinges. Oblivious to the fact that she was dressed only in her thin robe and nightgown, Jordan ventured down the path, following the narrow beam of his flashlight.

When she reached the parking lot she stopped cold. An enormous shape reared over the mangled frame of her little Fiat. Ben was shining his flashlight directly into the face of the creature, blinding it. He knelt, picked up a rock and chucked it at the animal. "Go on, Lily!" he yelled. "Get out of here!"

Deeply offended, the bear dropped something, turned and lumbered off into the woods.

"Damn!" Jordan heard Ben curse as he moved to inspect the wreckage. Gathering up the soggy hem of her robe, she hurried to join him. "Jordan," he said when he spotted her at last. "You shouldn't be out here. Go back to the cabin!"

"Oh, no!" she moaned when she saw the extent of the damage to her three-month-old car. The canvas roof had been ripped open, the window on the passenger side broken, and the entire door crumpled like the center section of an accordion. "Look at this! It's ruined!"

"Serves the owner right!" Ben fumed. "Somebody was dumb enough to leave groceries in the front seat. Of course the bear went after it."

"Ben!" she cried. "It's my car! I own it! What am I going to do? Just look at this broken glass—"

"You! You own it?"

"Yes."

"You left food in plain view?"

"Well...yes," Jordan stammered. "I meant to bring it in earlier...but I forgot—"

"Jordan! Of all the lamebrain things to do!"

"I don't see why you have to be so mean about it!" she countered, bridling at his lack of sympathy. "It's my car that's been damaged here, not that wretched old bear. I'm the injured party."

"You airhead!" He threw his hands up, walked a few feet away and then came back again. "What's between those beautiful ears of yours? Helium?"

"I'm an airhead? And what's that bear? Some kind of genius?"

"Lily is a very intelligent animal. And she was just doing her job—she was looking for food. And whenever you leave some in an inappropriate place, you contribute to the delinquency of the bears. Once they're successful at ripping off tourist food, they'll do it again and again, and any bear who becomes too much of a problem may eventually have to be shot."

"Oh!" she said, newly upset by this information. "I didn't know. How was I to know?"

"Well, it's done. You've put Lily's future in jeopardy by your carelessness tonight."

"Ben, I feel terrible." Jordan shivered.

"You should," he declared. "Your bloody car is probably covered by insurance and can be replaced. But Lily's a living, breathing creature and these are her woods. This is her home!"

"I'm sorry! What do you want me to do? Leave?"

"Maybe that wouldn't be a bad idea."

Jordan gave him a furious look. And then she sneezed.

"Oh great!" Ben sighed. "You'll kill Lily with junk food and yourself with pneumonia. Come on." Before she knew what was happening, he had picked her up and slung her over his shoulder. "Let's go."

"Ben, put me down," she insisted as he tromped down the path to the cabin, knocking the breath out of her with every step.

He paid her no heed. At last he deposited her unceremoniously at the front door. "Best go in," he said gruffly. "Get out of those wet things. I'll talk to you tomorrow."

"Don't bother!" Giving him a look filled with rage, Jordan stormed inside, shut the door in his face and bolted the latch.

CHAPTER FIVE

"I HAD A CALL from the garage in Visalia," Jordan told Hallie one sunny morning in late June.

"What did they say?"

"The car's ready. I can pick it up."

"Bravo!"

"Think you can do without me for a couple of hours? The Winklers are checking out today and they've promised to give me a ride to town...."

"Oh, please! Go! You've been such a dedicated little innkeeper these past three weeks I'm beginning to feel guilty for lying here." Lifting the knitting that covered her lap, Hallie gazed down at her own blossoming form and uttered a comic sigh.

"Well, you mustn't feel guilty!" said Jordan. "Not for a minute. You know I'm here to help."

"Yes, but I want you to have *some* fun, Mary Jordan! Why don't you take the rest of the afternoon off and go to a movie in town?"

"I don't think so."

"Or better yet, stop at Ben Gerard's place on your way back and let him know there're no hard feelings."

"Are you crazy?" Jordan rolled her eyes. "You weren't there, Hallie. You didn't hear all the names he called me."

"Oh, I'm sure he was plenty angry, but he's probably over it by now."

"Then perhaps he should apologize to me!"

Hallie shrugged and resumed her knitting. "Now, Mary Jordan. Don't get all puffed up and huffy. It was an unfortunate accident, but it's nothing for you two to start a feud over."

"There's no feud! I just think we're better off staying out of each other's way."

"Hmm."

Jordan eyed her sister with suspicion. "Why do you say 'hmm' like that?"

"Well, it does seem a pity. Here you are, attractive and single, and there he is, attractive and single. I thought you might keep each other company over the summer. Who knows?"

"Hallie McKenna Brundin, don't you dare play matchmaker!"

"Why not? I'm lying here all day long like a beached whale. I've nothing else to do. Besides it might be good for both of you."

Jordan was adamantly opposed. "I've just broken off an engagement. I'm not ready to see anyone else."

"Oh bosh."

"And if I were, I don't think it would be Ben."

"But he's so sexy," Hallie teased. "Don't you think so? I know I do. Those deep dark eyes!"

"I'm gonna smother you with this pillow."

"Ma-ry Jor-dan," Hallie sang. "Ma-ry Jor-dan—"

"Stop it! I don't happen to like Ben Gerard and he doesn't like me! If I stopped by his place, he'd probably have me shot on sight. Jordan McKenna. Corrupter of Bears."

Hallie laughed. "It's true. He does love those wretched old bears. Maybe too much. I think you should go over there and lure him back into the world of human relationships."

"Absolutely not!" Jordan raised the pillow and threatened her sister with it.

"Hullo." Pete poked his head in the door and regarded them both with an inquisitive expression. "What's up?"

"Nothing!" Jordan dropped the pillow into a chair and coolly seated herself. "Hallie's just going a little soft in the brain, that's all."

"It's true!" Hallie agreed. "Pete, I'm stir-crazy. I've been so good lately. Don't you think I could go downstairs for a while?"

"Uh-uh. You know what the doctor said."

Hallie sighed and plunked down her knitting in frustration.

"What?" Jordan wanted to know. "What'd he say?"

"The last time we saw Dr. Simon, he was very concerned." Pete's face held a look of seriousness that took her by surprise.

"When was this?" she asked.

"Two days ago. He thinks Hallie's being stubborn and foolish."

"Oh, Pete, I am not!" Hallie protested.

"Yah, you are. He says it's risky for you to stay up here in the woods, so far from everything. He says you ought to move into town so you can be near the hospital."

"Now don't start!"

"Hey," Jordan interrupted, "won't somebody let me in on this? I'd like to know the whole story."

Hallie made a face. "There's a conspiracy afoot— between Pete and Dr. Simon. They want to move me down the mountain and into some dumb apartment with a nurse I don't even know. Well, I'm not going."

"Hallie—"

"I'll be fine! I'll stay in bed and watch TV and knit a hundred thousand sweaters and do every blasted thing I'm supposed to. I promise! Girl Scout's honor!" She held up one hand in a solemn pledge. "But I won't be separated from you all."

"I'd come and see you," Pete offered, "every day." Jordan could tell he was truly worried.

"Look, if I stay up here I can be of some use. I can help Pascal plan the menus. I can balance the accounts. Otherwise I'd feel awful—sloughing all the responsibility onto you and Jordan."

"Hallie, your first responsibility is to yourself," Jordan interjected, "and to Pete Jr. or Hallie Jr., or whoever's in there. Don't worry about this place. I'm fully capable of planning a menu."

Hallie closed her eyes and shook her head slowly back and forth. Jordan remembered the gesture from childhood. Her sister could be very obstinate . . . once she'd made up her mind about something. "I'm feeling great," she insisted. "Better than I've ever felt in my whole life. I think Dr. Simon is being a teensy bit old-fashioned. I think you're all blowing the whole thing out of proportion. Now come on, let's talk about something else. Pete, don't you think Jordan is looking especially pretty?"

"Hallie—"

"Much too pretty to sit around here. I've been trying to persuade her to take the day off."

"Jordan's free to do as she likes," Pete said, frowning. "I came up to tell her that the Winklers are almost ready to leave. But Hallie, we have to discuss this sooner or later—"

"Later!" Hallie insisted. "We'll discuss it later. Now run along you two. Tell the Winklers goodbye for me and that we hope they'll come back and see us again soon!"

"You think it's important for her to move into town?" Jordan asked Pete as soon as they were out of earshot. She was disturbed by her sister's apparent refusal to deal with the situation.

"Sure," he agreed. "As I said, hers is a very risky condition."

"What could happen? Be honest with me."

"There's an awkward positioning of the placenta, and she could hemorrhage easily. She could lose the baby. Endanger her own life. That's why she needs to stay within minutes of the hospital."

Jordan frowned. "Scary," she said.

"Very scary."

"She simply has to go."

"I know. But what can I do? I can't tie her up and carry her down the mountain. She has to go of her own accord."

"If only she weren't so stubborn."

"Well, you know Hallie. She's always been self-sufficient. I don't think she can stand to be so dependent now—not even on those who love her."

Jordan nodded. "We'll have to convince her."

"You talk to her, Jordan. She won't listen to me."

"All right," she said, giving his hand a warm squeeze. "I will. As soon as I come back!"

The car was ready as promised. Jordan paid the garage and then decided to pass on the offer of an afternoon off, opting instead to return directly to the lodge. She was eager to confront Hallie, to reassure her sister that she, Jordan, was fully capable of running the place in her absence.

The fact was she liked her new role as temporary mistress of the inn. She liked the contact with people, the homey informality, the laid-back atmosphere. It was certainly a dramatic change from the intensely competitive world of Weinstein, O'Connor and Associates. And for the time being, she was content with it.

Of course she occasionally missed the glamour of city living. How could she not? She simply wasn't used to the early country mornings, the empty idle evenings. Often as she'd teased Scott about his preoccupation with the urban life-style—with dining out, with shopping and theater-going and all the rest—Jordan had discovered that she was somewhat addicted to it as well. When she'd scanned the papers and realized she was missing all the jazz concerts at the Hollywood Bowl, Jordan had felt a definite pang of longing for the pleasures of civilization.

But there were compensations.

Each day she awoke to the song of birds, a welcome relief from the cacophony of buses and cars and sirens that regularly greeted her in Los Angeles. She'd traded in her high heels for sneakers. And, one of these days, she fully intended to go out and explore the natural glory of the wilderness that surrounded her.

Purposefully bypassing Ben Gerard's log house in Ash Mountain, Jordan sped along the winding roads through redwood and cedar forests, past waterfalls and meadows as she drank in the sweet smog-free country air. And then before she knew it, she was home again. She pulled into the parking lot and stopped short.

Resting on the lawn like some monstrous prehistoric dragonfly was a large black helicopter. She stared at it in vague alarm. A helicopter? Was something wrong? Was there an emergency? Her thoughts went instantly to Hallie. Jordan stumbled out of the car and fell all over herself as she raced into the lodge and up the stairs to her sister's room.

"Hallie?" she gasped, throwing open the door.

Four faces turned to stare at her.

"Mary Jordan! Where were you when we needed you?" her sister chided.

"Are you all right?"

"Well, sure. Only we needed a fourth for poker. And since you weren't available, we had to draft Pascal from the kitchen."

Gathered around Hallie's bed, engrossed in a card game, were the French chef, Pete, and a plaid-shirted, jean-clad, ever-handsome Ben Gerard. Jordan blinked in bewilderment. "Hallie, there's a helicopter sitting on the front lawn."

"I know! Isn't it exciting? Ben just got his license and he came over to give me a ride. You know, break up the monotony of the bedside routine. Of course Pete said no."

"Of course," she murmured, aware that Ben's dark eyes were fixed upon her.

"Want to pull up a chair and kibitz?" Hallie invited. "We're having a great game."

"You think it's great," Ben drawled, "because you're winning. You've just about cleaned me out, woman!"

"It's true," Hallie gloated to Jordan. "I've taken twenty-three dollars and fifty cents off these suckers in the last couple of hours!"

"And ten of it was mine!" Ben complained. "I think you ought to start a trust fund for the kid. By the time he's here, you'll have enough to put him through college."

"Come on, one more hand! I'll give you a chance to win it all back!"

"No way!" Ben folded his arms across his chest and rocked back from the table.

"No way, Madame Hallie," Pascal echoed in his heavily accented English. "I must leave to prepare the dinner. Otherwise the guests go hungry."

"Oh all right," Hallie agreed reluctantly. "Ben, you're staying for supper, now. I insist."

Thanks a lot, Hallie, Jordan thought. She'd avoided the man's office only to find him snugly settled here at home, ensconced in Hallie's chintz-covered chair like a big black panther. Oh! That awful matchmaking sister of hers! Just because Hallie was bored and pregnant and everyone was worried about her, she thought she could meddle in other people's lives with total impunity. Jordan sighed and crossed to the window to gaze at the infernal bug-eyed machine on the lawn.

"Ben," Hallie was saying in her sweetest voice, "I was just thinking..."

"Yes, ma'am?"

"Since you've come all the way over here, and since Pete won't let me go up in the 'copter, maybe you could give Jordan a ride instead."

"Hallie!" Jordan gave her sister a discouraging look.

"She needs a little diversion! She's been stuck here in this lodge for the last three weeks working herself silly. Couldn't you take her out for a while? You've got lots of time before supper."

Ben glanced at Jordan. "I suppose I could," he said.

"No!" Jordan sputtered. "For heaven's sake, Hallie, you're imposing!"

"I am not." Hallie smiled a madonnalike smile. "Ben would tell me if I was, wouldn't you, Ben?"

He rose, lithe and lean, from the chair and stretched his arms lazily over his head. "What do you say, Jordan? Want to go up?"

"I don't know. I really don't think . . ."

"Right." He shrugged. "You're probably afraid of heights."

"I am not afraid of heights!"

"Good!" Hallie clapped her hands. "Then it's settled. Have a wonderful time, you two! Come back and describe it all to me later."

IT WAS ONE of those crystal clear Sierran afternoons. Each tree and rock, each blade of grass was sharply delineated, and the sky was so unbelievably blue it stunned the senses. As Ben brought the helicopter down to rest in an alpine meadow, he glanced at Jordan as if to see how she was taking it.

Jordan had ceased to breathe. Her eyes were wide and her knuckles white as she gripped the seat in certain anticipation of a crash landing. The flight had been exciting, she had to admit, but the descent frightened her. She was the same way on airplanes on the rare occasions she flew.

Ben smiled and shook his head. "Relax," he said. "I passed the test. I'm not going to kill us."

"I'll relax," she whispered, "as soon as we're on the ground. Don't make fun of me, Dr. Gerard."

"I wouldn't dream of it."

Her relief was audible when he cut the motor at last and the great whirring blades of the propeller spun to a stop. Ben slid out of his seat and crossed around to assist Jordan as she planted her two size-six tennis shoes once again on terra firma. "There," he crooned. "Safe and sound. What'd I tell you?"

She held on to his arm for a long moment. "I wasn't really scared," she explained defensively. "I do lots of risky things. I drive on the Hollywood freeway during rush hour. By myself."

"Wow."

"I've just never been up in a helicopter before," she said, bridling at the quiet mockery in his voice, "and after all, how do I know you're that good? You haven't had much experience!"

"Maybe not," he agreed amiably. "But at the moment, I'm the only pilot you've got, Miz McKenna. You can't get back without me. So watch your mouth."

Jordan frowned, then let go of his arm and turned to survey the meadow. "Where are we?" she asked.

Stretching away at their feet was a vast blue carpet of wildflowers.

"From the top of that hill, you can look out over the Great Western Divide."

"The Great Western Divide?"

"Yes, ma'am. It's just a short hike. Are you game?"

Thrusting her two still-shaky hands into the pockets of her slacks, Jordan took a deep breath and lifted her chin resolutely into the air. "Lead the way," she said.

What had possessed Hallie to try to play matchmaker? Jordan wondered as she strode through the rustling grass, trying to keep up with Ben's vigorous pace. She and Ben had nothing in common! Their worlds were diametrically opposed. He was a nature lover; she was a city sophisticate. He worked with his instincts; she had always made her living via her intellectual abilities. She knew he thought her a wimp and a scaredy-cat, but she wondered how well he'd fare in the urban jungle she'd once coped with on a daily basis.

An insistent bee was buzzing loudly about her head. Jordan closed her eyes and shook her hair, hoping to drive it away. The action caused her to lose her footing momentarily, and she stepped in an unseen hole, twisting her ankle. "Ouch!" she cried.

Ben looked over his shoulder to see what the matter was. "You okay?" he asked, frowning.

"Perfectly!" she assured him, despite the pain. She wasn't about to provide him with any more ammunition for his sarcastic potshots.

Apparently he accepted her answer. Without even waiting for her to catch up, he turned and tromped toward the hill.

He was better off alone! Jordan thought as she limped after him. He didn't need companionship. He was better off with his marauding bears and his memories of his perfect wife. Mary! If all reports were correct, Mary Gerard had probably been every bit as intrepid as he. An Amazon. A superwoman. Indifferent to bees. Invulnerable to gopher holes.

Jordan wondered if he missed Mary, if perhaps he still felt married to her in some way. Hallie had said that Ben had dated other women since his wife's death but that he never seemed to become deeply involved. Was he comparing every new woman he met to the ideal of Mary?

"Hey, McKenna." Ben had arrived at the base of the hill. Snapping off a long blade of grass, he chewed it thoughtfully. "There's something I've been meaning to talk to you about."

"What's that?" she puffed.

"You're a writer, aren't you?"

"I used to write advertising copy," she informed him as she reached his side at last. "You know, magazine ads, brochures, that sort of stuff."

"Have you ever tried anything else?"

"No, not really. Why?"

"I know an editor who works for a nature magazine." He named the publication. "He's been after me to write an article about the bears in Sequoia."

"Why don't you?"

"I hate sitting down at a typewriter! I don't have the temperament for it. It's agony just putting together some of these routine reports."

Jordan cocked her head to one side and regarded him with curiosity. "Are you asking for my help?"

"Yeah." He shrugged. "I thought maybe I would."

She laughed, a short staccato burst. "Well you've got a lot of nerve, fellow."

"Beg pardon?"

"The last time I saw you, you were incredibly rude," she said, reminding him of the occasion. "You impugned my capabilities left and right. You called me an airhead and a lamebrain...."

"Aw, hey, you're not still mad—" he scratched his head in bewilderment "—are you?"

"You bullied me around, you know. You threw me over your shoulder like a sack of meal. You watched that bear demolish my car and you never phoned or anything to check on the damage."

"You told me not to bother! You locked me out of the house!"

"That's no excuse!"

"Jordan...!"

"If you want help with that article, maybe you'd better ask one of the local geniuses—like your friend Lily!"

He stared at her. His expression was so intense, she thought for a moment that he might reach out and shake her. "Good grief!" he sputtered. "What do you want? An apology?"

Jordan indicated that this might be agreeable.

"It was your own damn fault! Everything that happened," he replied gruffly. "You know it was. But all the same...I'm sorry...about the car."

"Hmm." She regarded him through narrowed eyes. "Are you sorry about the name-calling and the rough stuff as well?"

"Not exactly."

"Well..." She turned her back on him and began to climb the hill. If he didn't have the good manners to apologize, that was his bad luck. "*I'm* sorry I can't help you with your article."

"Wait a minute!" Ben called. Now it was his turn to hurry and catch up. "Hang on, Jordan! Let's talk seriously now."

"I am serious."

"Jordan, please..." Much as he hated to admit it, he was close to desperate. He'd tried to write the confounded piece himself. He'd sat alone at his desk every night for the past ten days and come up with only a jumble of words and a sketchy outline. "I'm in a pickle. Come on, hear me out."

She'd reached the crest before him and plopped down on a large, sun-baked rock. "Nice view," she commented when he'd climbed up to join her. "What did you say it was?"

"The Great Western Divide."

"Fassscinating."

"You're a prissy little witch! You know that?"

"More names?"

"Okay, okay." Ben sighed. "You're not a witch and you're not an airhead," he began. "You're an intelligent, capable, grownup person and I'd like to hire you. I'll pay you. We'll split the proceeds fifty-fifty."

"Wow," she said, giving him her full attention at long last. "Just what sort of pickle are you in?"

"A couple of weeks ago I saw Dave, my editor friend. He was up here on a visit and we spent most of one evening sitting around, drinking Scotch and swapping stories. Well, around four in the morning, in a somewhat inebriated condition, I signed this . . . contract, promising to deliver the article."

"Oh, no! You signed a contract?"

"Yep."

Jordan stared out thoughtfully at the horizon and rubbed her sore ankle. In the distance, the blue-white mountains, snow-capped even in summer, stretched out in a magnificent jagged chain. "Then I guess you'll have to deliver," she said. "When's it due?"

"Two weeks from today."

"What!"

"Five thousand words. Warm, witty and neatly typed."

"Oh, Ben!" She grimaced. "That's not an article. That's *War and Peace*."

"You can do it."

"No," she protested, "I can't! Why, I've never written more than a few paragraphs at a time. My forte is short and snappy. Besides I'm retired."

"Jordan—"

"I mean it. I'm here to help Hallie and Pete at the inn. My hands are full. Can't you ask someone else?"

"Unfortunately you're the only writer I know," he explained. "Abby's in New York. . . ."

"I feel for you, Ben," she admitted. "I really do. But it's out of the question. I don't have the time and I don't know the first thing about bears!"

"I'll tutor you. I have all the information. I just don't know how to present it. Come on, Jordan." He took her hand impulsively and squeezed it. "Say yes."

Jordan took a deep breath. She could feel her inner resolve starting to weaken . . . just a bit. He was so persistent, and so darned attractive, with his plaid shirt open at the neck, his hair tousled and falling forward onto his brow. "It's really not that hard," she said at last. "You write the first draft and I'll look it over. Correct the spelling. Patch up any awkward sentences."

This failed to satisfy him. "I cannot put pen to paper and have it result in anything coherent," he insisted. "I'm quite useless that way. You've got to do the piece, Jordan. I need you!"

The panicked look in his eye told her that he meant it. He was probably every bit as stumped by the project as he claimed. There were people like that: knowledgeable and good at their jobs but nonetheless incapable of organizing their thoughts on paper. Funny, she thought. He was fearless when it came to the physical world. He flew helicopters over treacherous mountain passes, he was on a first-name basis with the local bears, yet the man was intimidated by a blank sheet of paper. She was just the opposite. Highstrung and finicky, afraid of all sorts of things, but confident of her literary prowess.

Jordan gazed at his hand, pressed so insistently against her own. She could sense the inevitable flow of warm sexuality begin between them. What would it be like to work with this man? To have him around on a regular basis? Was she ready for that? Was it wise?

"I'll have to think it over," she murmured, flustered. "I just don't know."

He withdrew his hand. Reaching into his pocket, Ben drew out a set of keys and turned them over in his palm. "Okay," he said. "Go ahead and think." He nodded at the rock upon which she was perched. "Are you comfortable?"

"Yes. Why?"

"Because we're going to sit here until you say yes."

"What?"

He jingled the keys and grinned. "As I said earlier, I'm the pilot. You can't get back to civilization without me."

"You've got to be kidding!" Jordan looked at him in amazement and then she laughed. "Are you under the illusion that you can strong-arm me into writing your article for you?"

"Oh, no, that won't be necessary. I'll just wait here until you've come to the right decision."

"This is ridiculous!"

"All I want is your promise, Jordan. Say the word and I'll fly you home."

"You're crazy. You're a crazy man."

"I've got a deadline." He shrugged philosophically. "I have no choice."

"Well, I'll never help you now!" she flared. "I don't like your tactics, mister. I refuse to be coerced."

Ben was silent. He made a small game of passing the keys from one hand to the other.

"You're so macho," she accused. "You make me sick. You know that?"

"Flattery will get you nowhere," he counseled. "'Yes Ben.' Those are the words I want to hear."

Folding her arms stubbornly across her chest, Jordan looked away. Two could play, she thought. He couldn't keep her there all night. She'd call his bluff and then she'd never speak to him again.

Minutes passed. From the tops of the surrounding trees came the soft, feathery sound of the wind playing among the leaves. A black-and-white bird swooped down to light on a swaying pinecone.

And then Jordan saw the bears.

A female with two cubs in tow was moving slowly through the underbrush. "Look," she whispered. Ben nodded, indicating that he had already spotted them. "Anyone you know?" Jordan inquired nervously.

"I don't think so. This place is pretty remote."

"What's she doing?"

"Giving them their bear lessons—how to find food, how to look out for themselves..."

The cubs were still quite small. It appeared that the mother bear was leading them down the slope, away from the spot where Jordan and Ben sat. Jordan breathed a sigh of relief. "They're awfully cute," she admitted.

"Down in the park," he began in a quiet voice, "whenever some cubs put in an appearance, everyone wants to fuss over them. We have a hard time dissuading the tourists from feeding them."

"I'm sure."

"It confuses the poor animals. Just imagine. One summer you're a baby and all the humans you encounter ooh and aah over you and offer you chocolate-chip cookies. Then you go off and hibernate for the winter and you re-emerge as a two-hundred pound adolescent. You're hungry for cookies, but this time your reception is a little different. You approach those same people who were so generous the year before and they run away screaming, 'Help, I'm being attacked by a bear!'"

"Is that how Lily got started on her reign of terror?"

"Probably."

"I'm sorry, Ben."

"For what?"

"The debacle with my car."

"You didn't know. People have to be educated, that's all. It's part of my job. To try to help save a corner of this—" he made a passionate sweeping gesture, taking in the mountains and the forests and everything that lay between "—earth before we manage to destroy it through our thoughtlessness, our ignorance, our greed...."

Jordan looked at him. Despite herself, she found that she was moved, and before she knew it she said, "Okay. I'll do it."

"What?"

"The bloody article."

He seemed surprised. "You will?"

Jordan nodded half wearily, half humorously, and pushed a lock of hair out of her eyes. She was a sucker for children and small animals and men with a mission. "But not because you pressured me." She shook a finger at him. "I'm doing it because I want to, you understand."

"Terrific!" He grinned. His whole face lit up with relief and she found herself thinking once again how attractive he was. Well, sooner or later she'd have to deal with her feelings for Ben Gerard. She was a big girl. She could handle it.

Couldn't she?

Later, when they were high above the trees making their way home in the helicopter, a thought occurred to her. "How come..." she asked him, raising her voice above the noise of the propeller, "how come those bears walked out of the woods at just the right moment? That's what I want to know."

"What?" he shouted.

"I'd said no to you and then those bears came out of the woods and convinced me otherwise. Is this some kind of Indian medicine you're practicing? Did you put in a request?"

Ben laughed and shook his head. "Just a coincidence."

"All the same—"

"Look!" he interrupted. "There's Pete standing on the lawn waiting for us. What do you suppose he wants?"

"What's the time? Are we late for supper?"

"I don't think so." Ben glanced at his watch. "He's waving his hands back and forth. Looks pretty antsy about something."

Jordan shielded her eyes and strained to see the figure on the ground. "Gosh, I hope nothing's wrong...."

"Hang on! I'm taking her down."

In a moment, he had brought the whirring machine neatly to rest on the green expanse of the Sierra Forest Lodge lawn. Pete, who had moved away to safety during their descent, hurried back and rapped impatiently on the fiberglass door.

"What's up, old buddy?" Ben asked his friend as he tugged at his seat belt. "Just a minute. Lemme get out...."

"It's Hallie," Pete told him breathlessly. "Ben, is there enough gas in this bird to get us to a hospital?"

CHAPTER SIX

THE NEXT SEVERAL HOURS were as frightening as anything Jordan had ever experienced. Ben and Pete bundled Hallie into the helicopter and took off immediately for the hospital. There was no room for Jordan and so she followed in the car.

All the way down the tortuous winding mountain roads, she gripped the wheel of the Fiat, white-knuckled, remembering her sister's ghostly ashen face. It was obvious that Hallie was in a great deal of pain. Jordan knew few of the details: Hallie had slipped, Pete said, while taking a bath...a minor accident...but enough to aggravate her already delicate condition.

Dear God, Jordan prayed. *Don't let her lose the baby.* And then... *Don't let us lose Hallie!* The love she felt for her sister rose up and choked her. Fear knotted her stomach. Before she knew it, she was speeding. She pulled over to the side of the road for a few minutes and willed herself to calm down.

At the hospital, there were more anxious hours. Dr. Simon, alerted by an earlier phone call from Pete, was with Hallie when Jordan arrived. For a time, it was touch and go. But finally Hallie's condition had stabilized and the crisis was avoided. At least for the moment.

"Thank God," an exhausted Pete said to Jordan as he collapsed beside her on the couch in the waiting area. "Now let's see if she maintains for the next several hours."

"Can I go in?" she asked him. "Can I visit Hallie?"

"Later," he advised.

And so the three of them, Jordan, Pete and Ben, whiled away the rest of the night, drinking tea and talking, all of them much too wound up to sleep. Ben arranged for a colleague to pick up the helicopter so that he could remain behind to lend moral support. Jordan was impressed by his concern for her sister and by the loyal way he stood by Pete.

At seven the next morning, they stumbled into the coffee shop in search of scrambled eggs and a dose of caffeine. Both Ben and Pete had shadows of stubble across their chins. Everyone was wearing clothes from the day before. *We look like desperados,* Jordan thought, *coming in out of the wilderness.*

"Boy!" Pete sighed, rubbing his eyes. "I was never so glad to see that twirlybug as I was last night."

"Whirlybird," Jordan put in automatically, but she knew at a time like this the last thing Pete was worried about was his English.

"We were ready to set out in the car," he continued, "and that's a long trip. What if—"

"No 'what ifs.'" Ben's voice was firm. "The important thing is we made it. Hallie and the baby are going to come through this okay."

"Right. Right." Pete nodded. "I'm indebted to you, Ben. I really am. You probably saved her life."

"A number of things saved her life. Timing, luck, the good doctor...not to mention Hallie's famous fighting spirit."

"Yes, well, I hope now she'll stop fighting me and move into that apartment like Dr. Simon advised. It's much too dangerous for her to stay up in the mountains." Pete drummed his fingers on the table. "You tell her, Jordan."

"I will," she assured him.

"She'd be minutes from the hospital. She'd have a nurse, someone to fix her meals..."

"Just wait till she gets a taste of this food." Ben put down a forkful of scrambled eggs and grimaced. "She'll go wherever you tell her."

By noon, Hallie was propped up in bed looking wan and ethereal and very unlike herself. An untouched breakfast tray rested on the table to her left. "Hi," she croaked.

"You gave us quite a scare," Jordan said softly as she reached for her sister's hand.

"But I kept my baby! He's still right here."

"I know."

"Thanks for staying." Hallie pressed her palm. "I'm really glad to see you."

"Not half as glad as I am...to see you." Despite her resolve, Jordan's eyes filled with tears.

"Now don't cry, Mary Jordan."

"I won't. I won't." She swallowed hard and tried to assume a more cheerful expression.

"How was your date with Ben?"

"Hallie!"

"I want all the details...."

Jordan shook her head in weary amazement. Her sister had almost died the night before and the first thing she wanted to hear about this morning was the results of her matchmaking. "It wasn't a date. It was a ride. It was fine. Come on. Don't wear yourself out talking about things that aren't important."

"Not important!"

"The important thing is you! Hallie, we all love you very much and we want you to carry this baby full term. You've simply got to move into that nearby apartment like Pete says...."

"Yeah, yeah..." Hallie managed a wobbly smile. "Did he take you some place pretty, Mary Jordan? Did he flirt with you just a little bit?"

"You're incorrigible. You know that?"

In the end, she'd related the whole story. Hallie had listened attentively to the part about the mama bear and her cubs. She'd been pleased that Jordan had agreed to help Ben with his article. And then without warning, she'd drifted off to sleep.

"There's no reason for you two to stick around," Pete told his friends when it seemed clear that Hallie was out of danger and holding her own. "Why don't you go home? Get some rest. Jordan, can you give Ben a lift to his truck?"

"Sure," she agreed. "Where is it?"

"In the Giant Forest."

As if by mutual agreement, they fell silent somewhere on the outskirts of town and remained so for the rest of the trip. After twenty-four hours in the buzzing, bustling chaos of the hospital, it was a relief. Jordan felt a bone-deep weariness pull at her like an undertow. When she glanced at Ben, she saw that his face was dark and inscrutable. He'd dropped the cheerful mask he'd worn for Pete's benefit and was allowing himself the luxury of his thoughts. She wondered what they were.

At last they pulled into Giant Forest Village, deep in the heart of the park. "Where to?" she asked.

"What?" He sounded distracted.

"Where's your truck?"

"Let's see . . . Take the next right . . . into that lot."

Jordan complied. "Ben, thanks . . ." she said hesitantly, stopping beside his vehicle. "Thanks for all your help. I—"

"Come on. There's something I want to show you." In one swift move, he had bailed out of the car and was striding up the path into the trees. Baffled, Jordan followed.

The trail led into a grove of redwoods—shaggy, cinnamon-colored and massive. The late-afternoon sun filtered through the high branches and turned everything a dusty gold. And it was so quiet. Jordan felt as if she were entering a great cathedral or an ancient Druid temple, some place sacred and cool and outside the ordinary passage of time.

"Here." Ben motioned her to join him. He was standing near the base of one of the giant trees, his powerful figure dwarfed by its towering presence. Jordan had to crane her neck to see the top.

"What's this?" she whispered and then self-consciously she cleared her throat. "I'm afraid to talk. I feel like I'm in church."

"It's a sequoia," he explained, "the biggest and the oldest of them all. I come here when I need to put things in perspective." He seemed moody, agitated.

She watched as he shifted his weight back and forth from one foot to the other.

He was wrestling with something, Jordan thought. He had been just as upset about Hallie as she and Pete had been. And now, even though she was better, he couldn't let it go. "Oh?" she murmured, encouraging him to continue.

"I call this tree the Grandfather. It's been here maybe three thousand years. It was old when Christ was born. It was alive when the Trojan horse was wheeled into Troy."

That's history, she thought. *What about you, Ben? Now?*

"It's the largest living thing on earth."

Talk to me, she wanted to say. *Tell me what's on your mind.* But no words came and so she reached impulsively for his hand.

In a flash, he pulled her into his arms and held her close. Jordan was stunned. The attraction she felt for the man flared up and made her dizzy. At the same time, she sensed his restlessness and a kind of implosive pain. Raising her head, she gazed questioningly into his eyes.

They were dark and hooded. For a moment, she thought he might kiss her. But then, just as abruptly, he let her go. "Hungry?" he said. "I know I am. How about some dinner?"

"Ben—"

"There's a great little restaurant near here. Good wines. Fresh salmon."

"Are you okay?"

"No!" He laughed. "I'm tired and I'm ravenous and I'm high on coffee. I haven't had anything to eat all day beyond some horrible scrambled eggs. Come on." Lightly cupping her elbow, he steered her toward the path. "Let's go."

THE CHARDONNAY WAS LIGHT and dry and Ben liked the way it felt as it slid silkily down the back of his throat. The salmon was grilled to perfection. The dining hall was rustic and graceful and comparatively quiet. And the woman beautiful.

All in all, it was a happy ending to a harrowing day. So why couldn't he relax?

He glanced across the table at Jordan. She was speaking animatedly, telling him a story about some crazy thing she and Hallie had done as children.

"Anyway," she was saying, "Hallie was convinced she could fly. She built a pair of papier-mâché wings and jumped off our garage roof. Landed in the azalea bush and sprained her arm." Jordan sighed and attempted to push her tousled hair out of her eyes. She seemed giddy from the wine and the lack of sleep and her rumpled appearance only made her look relaxed and all the more womanly in his eyes.

"We thought she'd broken it. She carried on so," Jordan continued. "But it turned out, she'd only scared herself and wanted to be held." She glanced at him. "Sometimes that's the best medicine, isn't it? A hug. A little human contact when you're feeling low."

He knew she was still trying to figure out what had happened between them earlier in the woods. He wasn't sure himself. All he knew was that he had a hole in his chest and he wanted to stuff her into it.

"What do you think, Ben?" she asked.

He should never have touched her! Never excited those expectations—in her and in himself. But the fact was he felt like doing a good deal more. Felt like taking her home and making love to her. All night. Losing himself in her again and again. Mentally he began to unfasten the buttons on the front of her blouse.

"Ben!" Jordan was demanding a response. "You're not listening. Are you?"

"Uh-uh," he confessed.

She cocked her head to one side and regarded him with a curious expression. "What's with you tonight? What are you thinking about?"

"Oh, a zillion things." He rubbed his brow. "The hospital, Hallie, Pete..."

"You were very good with him. You stood by him like a brother."

"I felt for him," he said. "But mostly I was glad it wasn't me, waiting around in that bloody corridor."

And then Ben felt it begin again. The nightmare. The one in his head. He closed his eyes as a host of unbidden images swarmed through his brain.

Mary was standing high above him on a ledge in Yosemite...she called his name...he looked up just in time to see her slip...her arms flailed wildly...then she tumbled headlong down the mountainside...and he was powerless to stop her fall.

He'd known her neck was broken the moment he'd held her in his arms. But he'd taken her to the hospital just the same and sat around in corridors as the doctors took their sweet time pronouncing her dead. Hospitals! He'd hated them ever since.

Hurriedly he took a sip of the wine, then downed the glass in an attempt to suppress the memory.

"You're thinking of Mary, aren't you?" Jordan asked. Her eyes were full of sympathy and suddenly he resented her for it.

"I always think of Mary," he said gruffly. "She was the best thing that ever happened to me."

"Do you want to talk about it?"

"Not particularly."

"It's hard to lose someone..." she ventured, despite his discouragement. "I know. But don't you think you'll ever marry again?"

"No."

"I see." Jordan hesitated for a moment and then turned her attention to her salad as if the profusion of lettuce and carrots was very interesting to her. "Well, I didn't mean to pry."

"What about you?" he queried. "Any chance you'll patch things up with old whatsisname?"

"Scott."

"Right. Scott."

"I rather doubt it."

"Then we're just a couple of bachelors." Ben filled his glass again, then raised it in a sardonic toast. "Here's to the demise of romance! We're better off without it. Here's to being clear-headed and practical and getting on with the rest of our lives."

Jordan stared at him.

"Aren't you going to join me?" he asked.

She shook her head.

"Why not?" He clinked his glass against her stationary one, pressuring her for a response.

"Because... I think that's just about the dumbest thing I ever heard you say."

Ben laughed. "Jordan McKenna. The expert. If you know so much, perhaps you'd care to enlighten me."

"I don't know the first thing! I made a botch of it with Scott. But I still believe that kind of love is possible. And necessary."

He shrugged. "Maybe it is for you. I've already had my turn. I'm not looking for another." *Best to nip this right in the bud,* he thought. If he gave in to his impulses, if he capitalized on the intimacy that was always on the verge of blossoming between them, and pursued her, it could only lead to disaster.

"Ben—"

"Let's talk about something else, all right? If we continue along this track, I'll probably make you angry. And I need you—to write that article."

Jordan sighed. "The article," she echoed ruefully. "The article. I said I'd help you and I will. If it's due in two weeks, I think we'd better get started. Tomorrow."

"I'll stop by. Bring over some books, my notes, such as they are, and a couple of photographs."

"Good enough."

"And perhaps you should come with me one day when I go out into the field."

"Perhaps you should learn how to write a decent sentence. A couple of paragraphs even. Then you wouldn't need anybody at all."

"Hey, are you mad?"

"No." She shook back her fair hair in the haughty way he remembered from before—from the days when they had been feuding. "Why should I be?"

"Because. You've got this rosy romantic balloon. And I threatened it with a pin."

Jordan raised her chin one infinitesimal degree. "My balloon," she enunciated in her best patrician tones, "has nothing to do with you, Ben Gerard. You don't affect it in the slightest."

"Well, good."

"All the same, it wouldn't hurt you to learn a few writing skills. I'm not going to be up here forever, you know."

"Right. Baby Brundin arrives, and back to the city you go."

"You'll have to write your next article yourself."

"Then I should watch you closely, Miz McKenna. See if I can pick up a few things."

Jordan nodded, then devoted herself to the remainder of the salmon. She was miffed, he thought. Well, it couldn't be helped.

The road back to the lot was a long and winding one. Earlier, when it was still daylight, Jordan and Ben had decided to leave the cars where they were and stretch their legs en route to the restaurant. But now, in the blackness of the moonless night, the distance seemed infinitely longer than she remembered.

The trees rose up on either side, ominous in the dark. Only by craning her neck and focusing on the stars, could Jordan establish a point of reference. The whole situation made her a bit uneasy, but she was loath to say anything to Ben.

He was the most perplexing man. She felt more and more drawn to him all the time, but it appeared that he was a dedicated loner. Hallie's attempt at matchmaking had been in vain and Jordan intended to tell her so the next time she saw her.

From the sound of his footstep, Jordan could tell he was keeping pace by her side. No doubt he knew these forests so well he could find his way around them blindfolded. The rotter! He shared none of her phobias nor did he sympathize with them. And now he was even whistling! They could walk right into a bear, Jordan told herself, and never see it coming. This was crazy.

At that precise moment she stumbled over a rock.

"What's the matter?" Ben asked in response to her gasp. "Did you trip?"

"No. Yes! Ben, I can't see a thing. How do we know we won't run into Lily or Blondie or one of your other furry friends?"

"Because we won't. Trust me."

"Trust you?" She laughed uneasily. "Why? Has Lily had a change of heart? Is she no longer raiding campsites and flattening sportscars?"

"Not exactly."

"Well?"

"She's behaved herself the past couple of weeks but I'm sure she'll strike again before the summer's over."

"Ben!"

"But if she were around tonight, I'd know it. Okay?"

"How would you know? It's impossible to see. It's impossible to tell where we're going. It's impossible to—"

"Hey," he interrupted her. "You said I needed to learn some writing skills. Well, you could stand to pick up a few survival skills. You're a hothouse flower, Jordan."

"I just wish we had a flashlight."

"It's only a little farther." He touched her elbow and indicated that she should turn right. "Here's the entrance to the parking lot."

"Good. You're gonna have to guide me to my car."

"It's forty yards ahead," he assured her. "We're in a wide-open space, so you won't trip over anything."

"Easy for you to say," Jordan scoffed. "I can't see a thing."

"Sure you can. You can see a little bit if you concentrate. And the rest is easy if you use your intuition. Go ahead." He released her elbow and stepped away. "Try it."

"Ben! Don't leave me. I swear I'm totally lost."

There was no response.

"Ben!"

In the distance, an owl hooted and she heard a soft flutter of wings. Jordan waited anxiously. But still he did not answer. For all she knew, he might have vanished entirely. Above her head, the massive trees creaked and groaned, swaying from their enormous heights.

"Ben, I confess. I'm a hothouse flower. I'm a wimp. All my faculties have atrophied from years and years of living in concrete. Please, help me find my car."

The hush remained unbroken. Jordan felt like a small child in the middle of a bad dream. The world was vast and silent and she was afraid of the dark. "All right!" she fumed. "You skunk! You bear lover!" Willing herself into action, she began to walk forward. She had no idea whether or not she was going in the right direction.

After a few minutes, she decided she had somehow missed the car. She'd gone past it. She was headed into the woods. Jordan extended one arm in front of her and felt for a tree or a bush. Then gingerly she took another step. The hoot owl cried again, startling her. She stumbled two steps backward and struck something big and obviously very much alive.

There was nothing to do but scream.

"Hush!" Ben caught her by the shoulders. "Hush, Jordan, it's me."

Turning, she threw her arms around his neck and clung to him for dear life. He seemed genuinely surprised by the intensity of her fear. "There, there," he whispered. "You almost made it. You were only a couple of feet away."

"Where's my car?"

"Right here." He tapped the metal hood with his knuckles. "See?"

"I can't see," she repeated, shivering violently. "I told you that."

"I'm sorry. I had no idea you'd manage to spook yourself so badly."

"I've always been afraid of the dark!"

"Give me your keys. I'll open the door and turn on the lights."

"No!" she insisted irrationally. "Don't let me go!"

"I have to. Jordan, sweetheart..."

She pressed against him. For all intents and purposes, she had simply ceased to think. It had been a long nerve-wracking day. She was exhausted and confused and emotionally spent and she wanted to be comforted by another human being.

"Good Lord," he groaned. "Jordan, I..."

It was such a short distance from his mouth to hers. She wasn't sure whether he'd bent down or she'd looked up, but in a moment they were kissing. Tentative and tender like a couple of kids.

Ben cupped her face in his hands and tilted her head backward. "Jordan..." he whispered. His lips were full and warm against her throat. "Jordan..."

She slipped her hands inside his rough cardigan and over the flannel-covered muscles of his back. He had an athlete's body. Taut and powerful and alive.

Suddenly, for the first time that evening, everything seemed to make sense. All their stalemated arguments, their nihilistic conversation, faded from memory, and she saw him simply as a man. A man for whom she felt something. A man she longed to know.

That was the fundamental truth of it.

After a moment or two they froze, suspended in their lovemaking, her forehead pressed against his forehead, each encircled in the other's arms. Jordan was aware of a powerful energy that had begun to build between them. She could feel their breaths mingling, moist and rapid, their heartbeats echoing each other in syncopated time.

"You have two seconds," he said, "to get out of here."

She waited.

And then in a swift move, his mouth came down upon hers, savage this time, demanding that she open to him. "Oh, Ben..." she murmured and his tongue was in her mouth. She arched against him, feverish in the cool night, as he plundered hungrily. His hands kneaded her shoulders, traced the long curve of her spine and cradled her hips, pressing them against his own. She could sense the fire banked there.

Why wasn't she afraid? Jordan wondered in what was left of her mind. She should have been, but she wasn't. The darkness was so complete. They were enveloped in the elemental blackness of it all, unable to see each other, able only to taste and smell and touch. She was losing all sense of herself and blurring into him. Her body was alive and singing, her fingertips vibrating like the hum of a thousand bees.

She raked them through the thick tangle of his hair, tracing the contours of his skull. His kisses were softer now and more luxurious. He teased and grazed and then withdrew, luring her to follow him.

Never in all her life had Jordan experienced such desire for a man. And he seemed to want her just as much. For all his talk about wanting to be alone, Ben seemed ravenous for her. How had he managed to hold all this back? She didn't know. She didn't know.

When she returned his deep kisses with an ardor that matched his own, Jordan heard him moan with pleasure. His fingers were tugging impatiently at the buttons of her blouse, and when he had undone them, Ben reached inside and with his rough woodsman hands cupped the fullness of her breasts.

There was magic in his fingers. She could hardly breathe, the effect was so intense. Clutching the fabric of his sweater, she struggled to keep her balance as wave upon wave of the most exquisite sensations rippled through her. "Ben..." she murmured raggedly. "Ben, I..." But when he took the delicate crest into his mouth, she was no longer capable of words.

Nothing like this had ever happened to her before. It was a revelation. She had never imagined anything this intense could unfold between a man and a woman. Her mind was spiraling outward into space.

"We're both crazy, you know," he whispered huskily in her ear. "Stone crazy."

"Yes!" she agreed.

"You're a glorious creature, Jordan . . . and I think you should go home."

She laced her arms around his neck and held him close. "Why?" she demanded.

"Because." He nuzzled the top of her head. "In another minute, I'm going to make love to you right here in this parking lot."

"Come with me," she said.

He hesitated. "Uh-uh. I don't think you know what you're saying. I think you're drunk."

"Not on the wine. On you."

He laughed and rocked her gently back and forth in his arms. "Okay. On whatever. You're smashed on lack of sleep and all the recent drama and half-a-dozen other things as well."

"What about you?"

"I am, too. I'm tipsy with it. I want you so much at this moment, Jordan, I can hardly stand it. But I just don't think it's a good idea. Not tonight."

"Afraid I'll regret it?"

"Maybe."

She sighed plaintively. Ben laughed again, then kissed her resoundingly all over her face. "Get in this car, will you? I'll see you tomorrow."

"Promise?"

"I promise."

Later, as the first light of dawn was illuminating the woods outside the windows of her cabin, Jordan realized she had not once closed her eyes. This was madness. It had been almost forty-eight hours since she'd slept. Flinging off the bedclothes, she pulled on a robe and went downstairs to see if she could rekindle the one log that remained in the fireplace.

Ben Gerard! The man had destroyed her equilibrium, and she was still reeling from their encounter. She was embarrassed and excited and she couldn't wait to see him again.

"Am I nuts?" she asked herself as she stuffed a sheet of newspaper and a few twigs under the half-burned wood and struck a match. "In love? Infatuated? What?"

She'd arrived home in a state of mental and physical disarray, glad that the cabin was empty. Glad there was no one to tease her about her starry eyes and her rosy mouth and the two buttons she'd fastened in the wrong order.

A shower hadn't helped much to cool his touch. A cup of warm milk had had no effect whatsoever on her noisy, clamoring mind. She'd lain there between the cool sheets in a state of unmitigated surprise.

"Who is he?" she asked herself over and over. "Who is this man?"

As the fire sputtered into life at last, Jordan rummaged through the drawers of Abby's desk and found a pad of paper. Curling up on the sofa with her legs folded under her, she began to write. What emerged—to her amazement—was a poem.

CHAPTER SEVEN

"JORDAN?"

She was dimly aware of a man's voice calling her name.

"Jordan, wake up."

Groaning, she stirred beneath the blanket and considered opening her eyes. Bother! She'd only just lain down for a short nap before supper. And now here was someone wanting her attention. It wasn't fair.

"Jordan, I've brought you some coffee."

"Hullo, Pete," she mumbled in a froggy voice. "What time is it?"

"Nine."

"You're joking."

"No, I'm not."

Jordan turned her head toward the window. "But it's still light out."

"It's nine o'clock Tuesday morning," he said, transferring the cup into her hand and securing her fingers around the handle. "Time to get up."

"What!" She was baffled. "Wait a minute."

"You've had a good long snooze. You must've needed it."

Rising to one elbow, she took a sip of the dark, rich brew. Pete's special espresso. Guaranteed to put life into a corpse. "Oh gosh!" Jordan grimaced. "What a washout I am! No good to you at all."

"Don't apologize."

"How's Hallie?" she asked anxiously.

"Hallie's fine. The hospital released her late yesterday afternoon and we moved her into that apartment."

"You mean she agreed to it?"

"Dr. Simon and I didn't give her any choice." Pete smiled. He was bright-eyed and clean shaven and he seemed more relaxed than he had been in some time. "I think she sees the sense of it. Hallie's stubborn but she's not stupid. She had quite a scare."

"I know! I know! I have to call her. I have to go and visit." Panicked, Jordan sat up, placed the cup on the side table and clambered out of bed in her rumpled clothes. How could she have neglected her sister! How could she have slept—what was it?—almost sixteen hours? Fumbling through the closet, she pulled out a pair of slacks and a clean blouse. "Excuse me, Pete," she said.

"Jordan, whoa. Calm down. I know Hallie would like to see you, but first there's some business that needs handling here at the inn."

She paused, disoriented. "What?"

"The supply man is arriving in a couple of hours. I'd deal with him myself but—"

"Of course! Pete! How could I have forgotten? Of course! I promised Hallie I'd manage her share of the load and I will! Just let me—"

"There's no rush," he insisted. "Calm down. You've got plenty of time. I didn't come out here to chastise you. I just wanted to see how you were."

"Out of it!" she exclaimed. "I'm really out of it!" Jordan laughed at herself as she sat once more on the edge of the bed and turned to finish the espresso.

"You were out of it last night, too," Pete told her. "I dropped by around seven. Called your name a couple of times. I even shook you. Nothing. You didn't blink an eye."

"I've no recollection at all."

"Ben said he tried the same thing."

"Who?" Jordan gulped.

"Ben Gerard. Remember? My friend?"

"Of course I remember Ben," she said. "He was here?"

"Yah, he was. I think he was expecting to talk with you."

"Oh?" She felt a blush creeping upward from her feet, setting fire to her insides and burning her cheeks. Jordan crossed to the window and fussed with the curtains, hoping all the while that Pete had not seen her high color. The morning sunshine flooded the room.

"He brought you a bunch of books. They're on the desk. He said something about you helping him with an article?"

"Right. I am."

Pete chuckled. "Apparently you wouldn't wake up for him, either. No sir. He hung out in the bar for an hour or so and then he went home."

"Darn!"

"He seemed kind of disappointed, too. I guess you guys have a lot of ground to cover, huh?"

"Yes," she mumbled. "A lot of ground."

"Okay!" Pete stood up and stretched his long legs. "I'm off. Pop over in a bit and we'll review that supply list. The Fourth of July is coming up and we probably ought to double order a few items."

"I'll be there," Jordan told him. "Just as soon as I'm presentable."

When he departed she slipped into the shower, groggy and flustered and fairly giddy with emotion. Ben had come! He had come by to see her just the way he'd promised! Only she'd missed him. She was a day late.

Jordan soaped herself from head to toe and remembered his caresses. No one had ever made her feel like that—ever! He'd put her in touch with a part of herself she'd never known existed. She closed her eyes and allowed her mind to dance. In the space of a second, she imagined their courtship. She married him in a forest chapel. She gave names to their children.

Stop it! Jordan seized the knob and doused herself with cold. *You barely know this man. Listen to yourself, Jordan McKenna, babbling like a schoolgirl. You're twenty-five years old. You're an adult. Where's your common sense?*

"Gone," she whispered as she wrapped herself in a fluffy towel and stepped onto the mat. "Gone." Drying hurriedly, she turned to brush her teeth. "He's a good man," she informed the mirror. "He's passionate about his work. He's loyal to his friends. And I've known him for almost six months."

"But how many conversations have you had with him?" the mirror argued. "You can count them on your fingers, can't you?"

"So what?"

"Jordan—"

"I'm crazy about him!"

"You're crazy. Period. Last week you couldn't stand him and now you're in love?"

"Maybe."

"And how does he feel?"

Jordan reached forward and traced a heart on the condensed steam of the mirror's surface. "It's special between us. He cares about me," she said. "He wants me. I know he does."

Three days later, she was not so sure. Ben had failed to put in another appearance and whenever she'd called to apologize for missing him the first time, there'd been no one home.

Her only contact with him was through the books and papers and photographs he'd left piled upon her desk. Everything she'd ever wanted to know about bears. And then some.

At night after the chores were done, Jordan pored over the material. He'd made a lot of notes. He'd even sketched in an outline of the article. And he'd included a couple of his early attempts to write it. They were amusingly dreadful.

But the outline wasn't half bad and soon she was able to get started. She figured she'd better; the final draft was due in less than two weeks. Ruefully Jordan wondered if he'd turn up in time to proofread it.

Where was he?

She sighed, stuffed the papers into a folder and dropped it into the lower lefthand drawer of the desk. Was Ben avoiding her? Had he thought it all over and come to regret his part in their moonless-night encounter?

Jordan shivered.

Perhaps he thought she was a pushover. After all, she'd virtually thrown herself at him—and not for the first time. Perhaps he thought she behaved that way with every Tom, Dick and Harry who happened by. Well, it wasn't true! She was finicky and hard to get. Except around him.

Or perhaps—and this was worse—perhaps Ben had compared her to that perfect wife of his and found her lacking.

Mary Gerard had been a paragon. Athletic and outdoorsy. Brave and profound. A match for him in every way. She'd even had an overbite, the kind he found sexy. Well, Jordan had no overbite, thanks to provident parents and five years of orthodontics. How could she possibly hope to compete?

In despair, she pulled a second folder from the desk. It contained all the poems she'd written over the past few days. There were now about twenty in all. Some of them giddy and hopeful. Some sensuous. Some loving. Some frightened.

After a little while she added another to the stack.

A week passed and still no Ben. Before she knew it, it was the Fourth of July. Traditionally this was a busy time for the Sierra Forest Lodge, and since the holiday fell on a Saturday this year, they were booked to capacity. Jordan was helping out behind the reservations desk, welcoming the stream of incoming guests, when Scott Townsend walked through the front door.

"Hi, Jordan," he said. "Long time no see."

"Scott!" She was flabbergasted. "What are you doing here?"

"Oh, I thought I'd come up for the Fourth. Spend the weekend." He winked at her. He was tall and tanned and as dapper as ever in his Giorgio Armani shirt and slacks. In his hand, he carried a single piece of expensive-looking luggage.

"But...but...you never take a holiday. You always work..." Jordan stammered.

"Maybe I've changed. People do, you know."

"Scott—"

"Want to show me to my room?"

"I don't have one! We're booked solid."

Undaunted, he scanned the book that lay open before her. "Here I am," he said as his finger came to rest beside a name. "Townsend. Room 218."

Jordan blinked once, then twice. There it was plain as day. The reservation had come in a week ago and she had simply failed to notice. "Two-eighteen," she repeated and handed him the key.

"It's really nice to see you," he crooned. "You're looking great."

She ran her hand through her tousled hair, which was pinned precariously to the top of her head with a big colorful plastic clip. "You're joking," she said. *What in heaven's name is he doing here?*

"No, I'm not. I've missed you, Jordan. I'm looking forward to spending some time with you."

Jordan hesitated, at a loss as to how to deal with the situation. "Gosh, Scott. I don't know. I'm awfully busy. This is the Fourth. I've a banquet to prepare. There's a softball game, a dance this evening. And I'm in charge of everything."

"That's cool." He smiled and juggled the key in his hand. "Don't worry. I'll see myself upstairs. But sooner or later you've got to take a break, right? Surely, the hostess is allowed a dance.''

"Who's the cute guy?" her assistant wanted to know when Scott had gone.

"An old . . . friend," Jordan mumbled. Of all weekends for Scott to show up! Why hadn't he called? Why hadn't he warned her?

"An old flame?" the girl teased. She was a college student Pete had hired for the summer, a big-eyed romantic kid.

"Kind of."

"Wow, Jordan, he's really neat-o keen-o. He looks like somebody in a magazine."

"I suppose he does."

"Nothing like the fellows around here, that's for sure!" She sighed. "Well, aren't you going to fill me in on the details?"

"No, Susie, I'm not," Jordan said. "Forgive me. I have to drop by the kitchen and check on Pascal. You can handle the desk for a while, can't you?"

"I guess so."

"Good girl. If anybody asks for me, you know where I'll be."

The kitchen was as much a madhouse as the rest of the lodge. Pascal was up to his elbows in fruit and flour. "Mademoiselle Jordan," he exclaimed. "The pies! I think I never get them done."

"Of course you will," she assured him. "I'll help. What do you need?"

"Another bag of walnuts."

"There're some in the pantry. What else?"

"Pecans. And could you bring also whole-wheat flour? I think I make one crust whole wheat—for the health nuts."

"A terrific idea," she said, encouraging him in her best boss-lady manner. "You're a peach, Pascal."

"No. No peach." He shook his head apologetically. "Peaches all bad. Blueberry, *oui*. Apple. Apricot. But no peach."

"I meant..." Jordan giggled, then gave up the explanation. "Never mind. I'll fetch the stuff you need and be back in a minute."

In the dim recesses of the pantry, she finally had a chance to catch her breath and collect her wits. What a circus! She was responsible for feeding and entertaining eighty people and here was her former fiancé showing up unannounced. It had been some time since she'd given him a thought. She'd been much too preoccupied with the absent Ben Gerard.

The whole-wheat flour, which Pascal seldom used, was stored in a bin on the top shelf. When she failed to reach it standing on tiptoe, Jordan climbed on top of a nearby crate. How much did he want? A cupful? The whole thing? Cradling the canister in one arm, she unscrewed the lid to see how much was left.

"Jordan?" Someone spoke from behind her. Instantly she recognized the voice. It sent a tremor rattling down her spine. She turned and dropped the canister. A pale cloud filled the room.

"Ben!" she said.

"Hi." He sneezed.

For a moment, they stood there in the hazy air, staring at one another.

He was dressed in jeans and a soft white shirt and
he sported a full week's growth of beard. Jordan
thought he looked beautiful. The flour was settling in
a fine spray over his dark hair and lashes. "Oh no!"
She laughed. "I've bleached you."

"I'll recover," he said, brushing it away with his
hands.

"Here. Let me." Grabbing a dish towel from a hook
on the door, Jordan began earnestly dusting him off.
Her heart was pounding like a hammer in her chest
and she could scarcely breathe she was so happy to see
him. Loosening the clip, Ben shook out her hair,
which sent a second gust billowing.

"What a mess," she sighed. "Oh, what a mess!"
She touched his beard. It was soft and springy. She ran
her fingers through his powdery hair and then, before
she knew what she was doing, she kissed him.

He responded but Jordan sensed a note of reserve
that made her pause and back away. Something was
wrong, she thought. Something was definitely wrong.
"So," she began distractedly in a brisk chipper tone,
trying to hide her embarrassment, "how are you?
Where've you been?"

"Out in the field," he said. "I've been camping for
the past week, checking up on a couple of bears."

"I see." Flustered, Jordan knelt and busied herself
among the shelves, searching for the walnuts. "Sounds
like a lot of fun."

"It was."

"I tried to call you."

"Oh?"

"Yes, Pete told me you came by," she continued
breathlessly. "I've gone through some of the books

you left. I've even knocked together a rough draft of the article."

"Wow."

"I'll show it to you later if you like."

"Great."

"There's a party tonight. A buffet and a dance. You're invited."

"Thanks."

Couldn't he say anything? she thought. She was feeling torn apart and all he offered her were words of one syllable!

"Mademoiselle Jordan!" Pascal called from the kitchen. "The walnuts, *s'il vous plaît*."

"Coming!" she shouted back. "Well," she told Ben. "I've got to run. As you can see, it's bedlam here. But stick around and later on I'll give you a copy of the article. Then you can tell me what you think."

"Fine."

Gathering up the nuts and what was left in the canister, Jordan quickly exited the pantry, leaving him alone amidst the settling flour.

The day continued at the same breakneck pace. She was in demand everywhere. There was a crisis at the reservations desk involving a mixup of rooms. There were lost children and crying babies. And in the afternoon, the softball game proved so rambunctious that everyone seemed to require patching up. Jordan exhausted the lodge's supply of Band-Aids and Mercurochrome on all the skinned knees and elbows.

But by the time evening arrived she was able to steal away to her cabin and rinse the flour and the dust out of her hair. Glancing at herself in the bedroom mirror, Jordan dressed hurriedly for the dance. She'd chosen a splashy floral sundress, chunky earrings and a pair of sandals. It was a simpler look than the one Scott had helped her cultivate, but then he wasn't her mentor anymore, was he?

It was Ben she was concerned about. She wondered if his sojourn in the wilderness had really been all that necessary or if he'd just wanted to put some time and distance between the two of them. "I don't know," she whispered as she fluffed the damp tendrils of hair around her face. "Maybe I'm imagining things." And then she remembered his restraint when she'd kissed him earlier that day. He was not a man given to polite kisses.

The band was just beginning to play. Jordan could hear the strains of a popular song floating through the trees. Fastening her sandals, she slipped out the door and up the path to the lodge.

The first person she encountered was Ben. He was standing on the front steps talking to Pete. "Hi!" her brother-in-law greeted her. "Hallie just called. She sends her love."

"Oh, I wish she could be here!"

"I'm going to drive down later tonight. Take her some pie and a couple of sparklers." Pete tapped the box in his pocket. He'd been handing them out to the kids. "It's sad to spend a holiday all by yourself. Ben, come on, take Jordan out and dance with her!"

She glanced at Ben tentatively, wishing her relatives would leave them alone, wishing everyone would stop matchmaking. She'd hoped he would ask her of his own volition.

"Jordan?" He reached for her hand. Well, what could she do but accept? At this moment she just wanted to be near him.

He swept her onto the floor of the big porch that surrounded the inn. It had been cleared earlier for dancing. A combo had been installed in front of the picture window and a number of other couples had already joined in the festivities.

To both her delight and dismay, the number was a slow one. Shakily Jordan rested her hand upon his shoulder as she sensed his, warm against her waist. "How are you?" he said.

A ripple of laughter escaped her. "Nervous," she confessed. "I'm very, very nervous."

"Why's that?"

"I feel as if I'm about fifteen years old! I don't know how to talk to you anymore."

He grinned his slow devastating cowboy's grin. But his eyes were still serious. "You're a lovely creature, Jordan."

"You think so?"

"Yep."

"Then why aren't you happier to see me?" The question was a direct one, but she had to know.

"Who says I'm not?"

"Ben!"

"Okay. Okay. I'm just a little concerned, that's all," he admitted.

"Concerned about what?"

"You. Me. The other night."

The air was cool against her flushed cheeks. All around them, couples bobbed and swayed to the music. "I haven't forgotten," she whispered.

"I should hope not! We almost made love in the middle of a redwood forest, for heaven's sake."

"Almost." She swallowed. "Almost seems to be the operative word."

"Jordan, don't be coy. You know what I'm talking about. There's something very combustible between us. A chemistry. A kind of sexuality. It's been there since day one and it certainly hasn't got any less intense."

Around the eaves of the porch, a string of amber paper lanterns fluttered like moths in the evening breeze. "Yes," she agreed.

"You're a very desirable woman." Ben took a deep breath and frowned. "You're passionate and you're sexy and I'm dying to go to bed with you. I've thought of little else."

"But?" She touched the furrow between his brows delicately with her fingertips.

"Jordan! There're some things to be considered. I . . . I don't want to deceive you."

"Then tell me the truth."

"Damn it," he growled. "Didn't you listen to anything I said the other night in that restaurant?"

She searched her memory. The restaurant was a blur. Everything paled in comparison to what had happened later. . .in the forest. That part she knew by heart. Detail for detail. She'd gone over it a thousand times. She'd even written poems about it. "The restaurant?" she said.

"Yes!"

Well . . . for one thing, he'd talked about Mary. *She was the best thing that ever happened to me,* Ben had said. *I always think of her.* Jordan swallowed as the words came rocketing back to her. He'd said no when she'd asked if he thought he'd marry again. And then, *I've already had my turn. I'm not looking for another.*

"Ah..." she began, "I believe you said something about...not wanting to get involved with anyone...." Her voice faltered and she swallowed once again. "But then...later...well, I guess I assumed you didn't mean it."

"That's what I was afraid of," he said. "Jordan, I don't want another long-term relationship. I really don't. And you have to know that—up front."

She was quiet for a moment as the knowledge seeped slowly into her consciousness. Ben was telling her that he couldn't love her. That even if he became her lover, he could never reciprocate those deeper feelings she'd already begun to have for him. "Oh," she said. The word rolled out of her mouth like a stone and thudded invisibly to the floor.

"I didn't want to deceive you," he added. "I wanted you to know the truth."

"Thanks," she said dryly. "I appreciate your candor. You're quite a noble fellow, Ben Gerard."

"Oh, come on, Jordan—"

"No, no, you are. You're a bona fide prince!"

"Jordan?" A new voice interrupted them. "May I cut in? I think this is my dance."

Dazed, she looked up to see Scott Townsend standing next to them. The ballad she and Ben had been dancing to had just come to an end and a new one was about to begin. "So it is," she agreed distractedly. "Scott, this is Ben Gerard. Ben, you remember Scott."

The two men shook hands and exchanged vaguely suspicious glances. Jordan was simply eager to break away from a painful situation. Fortunately the band had shifted to rock and roll and she was no longer obligated to talk to anyone.

Scott was a good dancer. He led her onto the floor and launched into a series of steps, some of which she didn't know, obviously the latest thing from the city. Jordan moved restlessly in a sphere of her own, lost in thought.

What a fool she'd made of herself! Spinning fantasy after fantasy while Ben was away. Writing all those poems. Believing he cared for her while she allowed herself to fall deeper and deeper in love. It was absurd!

The fantasies had been open-ended and they had all involved her settling down with Ben in some paradisal form of domesticity. That was the way her mind worked. That was what she wanted out of life—a good man... a loving lifelong relationship.

But he, on the other hand, saw a definite set of brackets around any possible encounter. It would begin here. It would end here. No strings. No regrets.

For him she was simply a passing fancy. It was Mary who remained the love of his life. The woman had carved out a niche in his heart and he would not allow anyone to take her place. That way he kept her alive inside of him. Forever.

Jordan glanced at the spot where she'd left him. He'd wandered away. Now he was at the buffet table, talking to an appreciative Susie. Jordan sighed. Heaven help her, but she was in love with him. And for her it wasn't just sexual. Her appreciation had developed slowly. The night in the forest had merely served to bring all her buried feelings to the fore.

What was she going to do? Jordan pressed her palm against the ache in her heart. Jealousy and hurt, anger and desire simmered and seethed in her chest.

"Jordan?" The music had ended and Scott was at her elbow. "Are you thirsty? How about some champagne?"

"All right," she said.

She accompanied him to the makeshift bar that had been set up at the far end of the porch. Scott handed her a glass of the pale bubbly stuff and she drank half of it in one gulp. "Easy," he cautioned.

"Hey," she replied testily, "I don't need any advice from you. We've been through this before, Scott."

"I know." He laughed. "Boy, have I regretted the day I first tried to run your life!"

She looked at him curiously. "What do you mean?"

"I've been doing a lot of thinking, Jordan. You know, you really shook me up when you left."

"I did?"

"Yeah. But you also did me a favor."

Jordan took another sip of champagne. Out of the corner of her eye, she saw that Ben had disappeared. "How so?"

"Well, I guess I've always been a controlling sort of bastard," Scott admitted. "But nobody'd ever given me any real resistance before. None of the women I'd dated."

"Oh?"

"You were the first."

"You don't say." She was amazed to hear him acknowledge such a thing.

"Sure. I'd always figured that I knew best and that everybody around me should be grateful for my superior opinion."

"Scott Townsend! Is this really you talking?"

He nodded. "It took losing something I really valued to make me sit up and take a long hard look at myself."

Jordan was impressed. Scott was only the most egocentric person she'd ever known and for him to come to this sort of realization was nothing short of astounding.

"I can tell you," he continued, "I wasn't too pleased with what I saw. I didn't treat you very well, Jordan. I think I owe you an apology."

She stared at him dumbfounded. "I never, never thought I'd hear you say something like that."

"Well, there's more. I've got a lot more to say to you and I hope you'll hear me out."

The man seemed sincere, not just the old slick Scott with his smooth talk and his ready smile. Jordan felt herself moved to listen to his story . . . but just then a sixth sense told her that Ben was nearby.

In fact, he was standing behind her. "Excuse me," he said. "Jordan? If you don't mind, I think we have some business to discuss."

Turning, she registered the quiet intensity in his voice. "Business?" she said.

"The article. You were going to show it to me."

"Oh! Yes. Of course." She felt as if she was being pulled in several directions all at once. "Scott, you'll have to pardon me." She reached out and clasped his hand. After all, he was standing there with his face wide open, looking so unaccustomedly vulnerable. "We'll talk later. I promise."

"All right," he agreed.

Ben took her elbow and guided her through the maze of dancing couples. When at last they reached the front steps, he spoke. "What's whatsisname doing here?" he said.

"Scott. Scott Town-send," she enunciated slowly.

"I can never remember."

"That's funny," Jordan remarked. "You can always remember the names of bears. Is it just people that you have such a hard time with?"

He ignored her dig. "What's he doing here, Jordan?" Silently, she descended the staircase and preceded him down the path toward the cabin. "Did you invite him?" Ben pressed.

"He showed up on his own. He's a guest."

"Well, how long is he going to stay?"

"I don't know."

Ben snorted. "What are you trying to do, Jordan? Make me jealous?"

She twirled around to face him. "You?" Jordan had to laugh. "Jealous? Why should you be jealous? You don't get involved!"

For a moment they stared at each other. And then he seized her, entwining her hair in each fist, and pulled her to him in a rough kiss. "Ben!" she gasped. But he was kissing her again, hungrily, possessively.

Jordan pushed against his chest with both hands. She was furious with him. How dared he! After what he'd said how dared he treat her as if she was his private property?

He didn't love her. He didn't give a damn about her. For him she would always be an afterthought. Someone to enjoy for a day or a week, a month perhaps, and then forget. Just as she sensed her own traitorous body beginning to weaken and succumb to his embrace, Jordan managed to pull free. "Leave me alone," she said hoarsely. "I don't belong to you."

Looking like some fierce forest animal, Ben took two steps toward her. And then he stopped. "I must be crazy," he said. "I must be out of my mind."

"Halloo, Ben!" Pete was calling from the top of the stairs. "Is that you out there?"

Wearily, he rubbed his forehead with the palm of his hand. "Yes," he answered, then louder, "Yes!"

"There's a call for you from the ranger's station. Seems some bear has kicked up a real ruckus over toward Grant Grove. I think you'd better get over there right away."

CHAPTER EIGHT

IT WAS LILY, of course. The three-hundred-pound femme fatale had struck again, just as he'd predicted. She'd happened upon a Fourth of July cookout and decided she ought to be invited.

Bears, as Ben well knew, were excellent actors. They were fully capable of convincing an unsuspecting human audience that they were about to attack. They'd wuff and growl and paw the ground in hopes of scaring the wits out of everyone. Then when the premises were vacated, they'd help themselves to the food.

He had been trained to tell the difference between a truly threatening bear and one that was merely bluffing. But unfortunately the party in Grant Grove did not share his expertise. When Lily appeared and ran through her customary performance, the half-dozen semi-inebriated men and women panicked and rushed screaming to the authorities.

And now Lily's life was in jeopardy.

Because of her scandalous record and the considerable amount of property damage attributed to her over the past two summers, it was highly likely that she might be tracked down and shot. Ben felt sick. He liked Lily. She was a pain and a nuisance but she was just a silly old bluffer who'd never harmed a human being in her life.

Well, there was nothing he could do about the situation tonight. By the time he'd arrived in Grant Grove the hullabaloo had been over. "Sorry to drag you away from your party," the ranger had said apologetically, "but it was that damn bear again, that reddish one . . . Lily."

"Are you certain?" he'd asked.

"Absolutely positive. She had her ear tags. And besides, I recognized her. I've seen her before."

Ben sighed. "What's the damage this time, Joe?"

"Boy, she made a real pig of herself. Six T-bone steaks and a German chocolate cake."

"Whew!"

"She left the potato salad though."

"That's not going to win her much sympathy at headquarters, is it?"

The ranger shook his head regretfully. "Nope."

After conversing for a while and casing the scene of the crime, they parted company. Ben climbed wearily into the cab of his truck and glanced at his watch. It was almost eleven o'clock. He really ought to get to bed and catch some sleep. Then he could be up bright and early the next morning to plead Lily's case before the board.

But halfway home, he found himself taking a detour. As if drawn by some magnetic force, Ben turned off the main road and headed down the lane that led to the Sierra Forest Lodge. Jordan! He had to talk to her. No matter how late the hour, he had to see her again.

She was becoming an obsession. When he looked back over the events of the past week, he scarcely recognized himself.

The incident in the forest had shown him how little control he had over his impulses. He'd nearly taken the girl right then and there. She'd been so sensual, so wonderfully responsive. He'd had to call upon every ounce of willpower he possessed to send her home.

The next day fortune had intervened in the form of exhaustion. He'd gone to see her and she'd slept through his visit like the princess in the fairy tale. Standing at the foot of her bed, amused and entranced, Ben knew that he'd been spared a second time.

In hopes of regaining some perspective, he'd trekked deep into the wilderness. Spent a week with his old pals, the birds and the bears. It had helped—a little. At night, he'd lain under the clear bright stars and gone over and over the pros and cons of his relationship with Jordan. He was deeply attracted to her. But he couldn't claim her. His profound doubts about his ability to encompass another long-term relationship were still much too great. Finally the conclusion he'd come to was this: he couldn't stay away but he could at least tell her frankly about his conflict.

And this evening he had tried to do just that. But it'd all come out so badly!

Unable to give voice to the complexity of his feelings, he'd managed to offend her. What was more, he'd become wildly jealous of Townsend and made a fool of himself. And now Jordan was furious with him. Ben felt he had to do something. Explain his behavior. Open his heart to her.

Pulling into the parking lot, he brought the vehicle to a stop and stepped out.

"AFTER YOU'D GONE," Scott was saying, "I called you every name in the book."

"I can imagine," Jordan murmured. They were sitting on the front steps of her cabin, enjoying the night air. After the dance, she'd allowed Scott to escort her to her door. She hadn't forgotten her promise to hear him out. After all, they'd been engaged once; she felt she owed him an audience. If clearing up the past could help them to forgive each other and be friends, she was all for it.

"No one had ever walked out on me before. It was a tremendous blow to my ego!" He shook his head and uttered a self-deprecating chuckle. "And what a tremendous ego it was!"

"The Goodyear blimp," she suggested.

"A seven-forty-seven!"

"All right," she agreed. "If you insist."

"I was outraged," Scott continued. "I thought you were throwing away your career. I thought you were wrecking our future...." He gestured expansively. "I blamed you for everything, Jordan."

"I know."

"Poor baby." Reaching over, he pulled the cardigan sweater closer around her neck to ward off the evening chill. "I really gave you a hard time, didn't I?"

"I got through it."

"I know you did," he acknowledged. "God knows I tried to put it all behind me! I tore up your pictures. Dated other women. Bought a new car. Worked so hard at the office that I was promoted again."

"Congratulations."

Scott shrugged off the compliment as if it really didn't matter. "Nothing seemed to make me feel any better. I was a wreck. I was setting myself up for some kind of nervous breakdown. Finally I went to see this psychotherapist."

"Scott, you don't mean it!" Jordan exclaimed softly. "You've always been opposed to that sort of thing."

"At that point I was ready to try anything. I met with the fellow a couple of times and then I signed up for this weekend group-encounter session at his office in Santa Monica."

Jordan found it hard to believe. The Scott she'd known had insisted upon doing everything himself. He'd made relentless fun of all the various therapies that were readily available in a city like Los Angeles.

"And do you know what?" he asked her.

"What?"

"Everybody in the group told me the same things you did."

She had to smile.

"That I was a workaholic, that I wanted to control everybody else, that I was a smooth talker, superficial..."

"Sounds like they got your number."

"Yeah." Scott sighed. "Yeah. Are you ever going to forgive me, Jordan?"

She took in his bright eyes and his contrite boyish expression. "It was probably my fault as much as yours," she said.

"How so?"

"Oh," she began thoughtfully, fingering the buttons on her sweater, "I played right into the whole thing. When we first met, I was mixed up and lonesome. I was looking for someone to tell me what to do."

"And there I was."

"Exactly."

"But pretty soon you started to grow up," Scott offered, "and I wouldn't let you. I wouldn't hear of it." He winced. "Well, I can tell you, things are different now, Jordan."

"I think perhaps they are." She patted his arm. "I think perhaps that therapist did you some good."

He nodded. "I don't claim to have changed my whole personality overnight. That would be ridiculous. I'm still ambitious and I still like having things my own way. But at least now I'm willing to listen."

"That's great, Scott."

"Jordan..." He hesitated. "I know I've put you through a lot, but I want you to think about giving me another chance."

She'd been wondering if he might be leading up to something like this, but she hadn't been at all sure. Now that he'd proposed the idea, Jordan didn't know what to say. "I..." she began awkwardly, searching for a response. "I don't..."

"I just want you to think about it," Scott insisted. "And when you're ready to come back to the city—"

"I'll be up here for a while yet! I'm committed to stay until Hallie has her baby."

"Of course," he agreed. "I won't push you. I swear I won't."

"Scott, there's—" But how could she tell him about Ben when it was doubtful whether she and Ben had any relationship at all?

"Oh!" he interrupted. "Speaking of the city, did I tell you? About the Adonis campaign?" He seized her hand excitedly.

"No. What?"

"It's an outrageous success! Your ads are on billboards all over the place. Not to mention the magazines! Haven't you seen them?"

She looked at him blankly. "Up here we're a couple of months behind the times," she explained. "The magazines in the lobby are from January."

"Well, girl, get yourself to a newsstand. The coverage is fabulous."

"Are you serious?"

"Sales are booming. Bicknell is ecstatic. He's singing your praises all over town."

"Bicknell?" Jordan was nonplussed. "Bob 'the Ogre' Bicknell?"

"The very same. He dropped by the office the other day, trying to find out where you were. Weinstein and O'Connor are stalling. They don't want to tell him you've quit. They're afraid they'll lose him. I think they pretended you were on vacation. In Europe."

"Those old buzzards."

"Don't be surprised if they drive up here themselves and try to talk you into coming back."

Jordan began to laugh. "I can't believe it! It's so absurd! I pulled my hair out over that campaign. I almost lost my mind."

"Isn't it amazing," Scott said, chuckling along with her at the irony of the situation, "how things turn 'round?"

BEN HEARD THE VOICES and the sounds of merry-making when he was halfway down the trail to Jordan's cabin. Well, he assumed, the party wasn't over. Too bad. He'd hoped to find her alone.

But when he saw her sitting hand in hand on the front steps with Townsend and laughing, he was so jealous he could hardly contain himself. For a moment, he stood there, half in light, half in shadow, as the unfamiliar emotion laid waste to his nervous system. And then he turned to go.

It was too late. She'd spotted him. "Ben!" Jordan said, rising to her feet.

He slowly pivoted to face her.

"What happened? With the bear? Was anybody hurt? Are you okay?"

"Sure," he said gruffly, digging his thumbs into the pockets of his jeans. "Everybody's fine . . . except Lily."

"Lily! What kind of trouble has she got herself into this time?"

"I don't think you really want to know." He frowned. "Look, I'm sorry to have disturbed you. I'll catch up with you another time."

"Of course I want to know," Jordan insisted. "I've been working on that darn article every day for the past week. I've used a couple of stories about Lily. Is this something I should include?"

"Well," he began reluctantly, "I think she's committed one offense too many. I think her number may be up."

"Oh, no! They're not going to shoot her?"

"It's a possibility. Unless I can convince the board to let me try something else."

"Such as?"

"I'll ask for permission to relocate her," Ben explained. "We could capture her, sedate her and then transport her to some remote point in the back country of King's Canyon."

"Would that work?" Jordan pressed.

"Maybe. Maybe not." He glanced at Townsend, then made another move to go. "We'll have to see. Good night. I'll keep you posted on what happens."

"Good night," Scott echoed, obviously glad to have him out of the picture, "and good luck."

"Ben!" Jordan ran after him. "Wait!" At the touch of her hand on his shoulder, he froze in his tracks. "Won't you please look over that article? I was just about to show it to you when you left."

"Right," he said. "Give me a copy. I'll take it along."

"I'm afraid it's all in longhand. But you can go inside and read it at my desk. It won't take long."

"It's late, Jordan."

"It's due awfully soon," she urged. "And I've been waiting a whole week for your opinion. I can't proceed without it."

Ben hesitated. He was afraid if he stood there much longer arguing with her, he'd lose his temper. "Okay," he growled. "Where is it?"

"In the lower lefthand drawer of the desk. Let me know when you're done."

Tromping past the bewildered Townsend, Ben stormed into the cabin and shut the door.

Lit by a single lamp, the place was welcoming and cozy. Ben looked around the room. Everywhere there was evidence of Jordan's occupancy; her flowers on the table, her books piled on the floor, her ridiculous size-six tennis shoes parked in front of the fireplace. Muttering irritably to himself, he crossed to the desk. When he saw that she'd left her shawl draped over the back of the accompanying chair, Ben scooped it up. The subtle scent of her assailed his senses and he chucked it across the narrow space where it landed in a heap on the sofa. Lower lefthand drawer, he repeated silently. Sliding it open, he pulled out a folder and sat down to read:

After the rains were over
When the sun came out at last
You appeared in my heart like a bud
Ripe and flowering and full of perfume
Concentric circles
Mystery within mystery within.

And my inner gardener
My sixth trickiest sense
Tells me that the sap of you
Is as sweet as home
As quick as light.

I try to ignore you
Bury you, damn you
Weed you out of my mind forever.
And still you sing on
Like the wind, like the rain
Like the pulse in my veins.

Adversary, lover, my soul's bull's-eye.

What the hell was that about? Ben asked himself.

What did that have to do with wildlife preservation? He read it over a second time. And then he realized. It was a love poem. A heartfelt one. Lifting the sheet and laying it to one side, he glanced at the pages that followed.

There was no article here. The folder was stuffed with poetry. Had Jordan written it? It appeared to be her hand—a graceful, flowing script.

Fascinated, he perused another poem. And then another. They were very affecting. Moody. Sensuous. Full of emotion. The lady was talented. And, it appeared, she was also very much in love. With somebody.

"I'M AFRAID I have to say good-night, Scott," Jordan told her ex-fiancé in hopes of getting him to leave.

He glanced at the lighted window of the cabin. "Burning the midnight oil, huh? Even on a holiday?"

"You know. Deadlines."

"Who's the scientist, Jordan? Anybody special?"

"A friend," she said noncommittally.

Rising to his feet, Scott reached for her hand. "I love you," he declared. "Don't go falling for anyone else."

"Scott—"

"I know. I know. I promised I wouldn't pressure you and I won't. But will you write to me? Let me know what your plans are, when you've made some."

"Of course."

"It was good seeing you again, sweetheart."

"And you."

Reluctantly he kissed the back of her hand and bid her adieu. Jordan leaned against the door frame, snuggling into her sweater as she watched him disappear up the trail. She'd been grateful for their talk. It had helped to dissipate any residue of bitterness lingering between them. That was good. She felt the lighter for it. She'd never believed in hanging on to a grudge.

But as to whether there could ever be anything more between Scott and herself, Jordan didn't know. At present, she was so ridiculously in love with Ben that it was hard to consider anyone else.

Not that there was any future in that direction! Ben had made his position clear. He'd really spelled it out for her. *I don't want another long-term relationship. I really don't. And you have to know that—up front.* The words came echoing back and stung her all over again from the inside.

Wasn't it crazy?

Here was Scott, offering her everything she'd ever wanted.

And then there was Ben, offering her nothing—except the possibility of a painfully brief and doubtlessly self-destructive affair.

No one, it seemed, was destined to be happy. They were all chasing one another in a fruitless, frustrating chain. Scott loved her. She loved Ben. And Ben...loved Mary. The man was married to a ghost! He was still devoted to his late wife and he could not bring himself to let her go.

Jordan rubbed her forehead. She hated feeling jealous like this. It was not that she resented Ben for having loved his wife. But did he have to cut himself off from all the love *she* had to give?

Oh, he might desire Jordan. She did, after all, have the singular advantage of being flesh and blood. But he would never never allow himself to care for her the way she'd come to care for him.

And knowing this, how could she allow herself to succumb to the great temptation of an affair? She'd be devastated when it was over. Jordan knew she'd be. Somehow—God knew how—she'd have to resist. And he must never guess how much she loved him.

The one saving grace in all of this, Jordan reminded herself, was the fact that Ben did not know the extent of her feelings. She'd had no chance to tell him.

All he knew was that some wildfire had swept over them one night in a forest. Something inexplicable and hot and fierce... but groundless. And brief. And ultimately forgettable.

Well, let him think that! She'd acknowledged as much already. Let him think her passionate, and a little wanton. He didn't have to know just how deeply he had touched her.

Inclining her head against the door, Jordan listened for some movement within the cabin. What was taking Ben so long? Surely he'd read the article by now. Curious, she turned the knob and stepped inside.

He was sitting at the desk with his back toward her, forehead propped in his hands, poring over the material. "Well, Dr. Gerard," she said, hoping to open the conversation on a professional note, "what do you think?"

"I think... it's remarkable."

"Really?" Jordan hadn't expected such a positive reaction. After all, she was a novice in the field. She'd just begun to research the subject. And Ben was an expert. "That's great. It's only a first draft, you know."

"You write very well."

"Thanks." She seated herself in a nearby chair, eager to hear his comments. The sooner the work was finished, the less time they'd have to spend together. "Are . . . are you almost finished?"

"I've read the whole thing twice."

"I thought you were taking a long time!"

Closing the folder, Ben turned slowly to face her. Jordan thought he looked a little strange. Beneath his dark brows, his eyes were positively smoldering. Apparently the sad dilemma over Lily was still very much on his mind. "Jordan, why did you show me this?" he asked.

Now she was confused. "Well," she began, "I thought it was high time. Don't you? I mean—"

"Who is it about?"

"Ben! What do you mean?"

"Who's the subject?"

"Why . . . Lily . . ." Jordan made a random gesture. "Blondie . . . good old *Ursus americanus.*"

He pulled a sheet from the folder and read the first line. Jordan felt her heart contract. It was a poem, one of the many she'd written to him. "Where did you find that?" she gasped.

"Lower lefthand drawer."

Instantly she was on her feet. "Can't be!" she cried. "Can't be!" Racing to the desk, she threw open the bottom drawer and pulled out the folder containing

the bear manuscript. "There!" Jordan exclaimed.
"There's your wretched article!" Slapping it against
his chest, she snatched up the poems and stumbled
back to the wall.

Ben stared at the new material. "Jordan—" he began.

"How could you have gone through my stuff?" she
accused, humiliated. "How could you?"

"It was on the top. I thought you meant for me to
read it."

"Well, I didn't!" Jordan hugged the folder. She was
on the verge of tears. "Now take the damn manuscript! Take it and go home!"

"We have to talk!"

"We'll talk tomorrow!"

"We'll talk right now!" Ben was adamant. "I want
to know. Who is the man in those poems?"

"It's none of your business!" She turned away from
him, trying to hide her face. If he hadn't guessed already, one look into her eyes would answer his question.

"Jordan!" He caught her by the shoulders. "Is it
me?"

"No!" she lied.

"Is it?" Ben was shaking her gently, insistently. The
nearness of him was enough to make her want to
throw her arms around his neck and confess the truth.
"Is it?"

"Are you out of your mind?" she flared. "What a
notion! What conceit!"

"Jordan—"

"Of course they're not about you! I...I wrote them
a long time ago...about someone I loved...."

"Townsend?"

"They're my personal property and you had absolutely no right to read them! How could they have anything to do with you? That should have been obvious from page one!"

"Did you write them about Townsend?"

"Let me go! I don't have to answer to you, Ben Gerard!"

He shook her again, hard this time, and the poems went scattering like leaves in a whirlwind. "What kinds of games have you been playing with me, Jordan?"

"What?"

"That night in the forest? What the hell were you doing?"

"It was fun." She made her voice sound hard, careless. "I had fun, didn't you?"

"And today? Tonight? Were you just having fun with me? Hoping to make Townsend jealous? Playing one of us off against the other?"

"Go home, Ben!"

"Have you got yourself engaged to him again?"

His fingers were digging into her forearms, hurting her. Angrily Jordan flung herself loose and stepped away. "He's better for me than you!" she declared. "He loves me. He wants to marry me."

Speechless, Ben stood stock-still and stared at her.

"Why shouldn't I choose him?" she continued wildly. "You don't care about me. You're not capable of it. I think you're the one who's playing games. Acting as if you own me when there's nothing between us at all."

"Nothing?"

"Oh, I don't deny the chemistry, as you call it. But I think that's all it amounts to."

"Jordan—"

"Go home, Ben!" she cried. "This has all been a mistake. Let's forget what happened that night. It was stupid and it's over. We're simply no good for each other. Now please! Go home!"

CHAPTER NINE

IT WAS INEVITABLE that she spoke to him again. After all, they had a contract to fulfill. Two days later in the afternoon, Ben showed up at the lodge as Jordan was going over the books in the office. "Here," he said, unceremoniously dropping the manuscript before her on the desk. "I made a few notes."

She glanced at him. He looked tired and unapproachable—but more handsome than ever. He'd shaved off the beard and his cool lack of expression served to highlight the high Indian cheekbones and the mouth she loved so well.

"Good," Jordan murmured, flipping through the pages. "I trust everything was basically satisfactory."

"You're a real pro."

"Thanks. I'll type this up tonight and then we can put it in the mail."

"Don't bother." There was an edginess in his voice. "Dave Buchanan, my editor friend, will be here on Friday. I can give it to him in person."

"Oh?"

"He's driving down from San Francisco with a photographer. They're hoping to document the capture and transfer of Lily. If the pictures turn out well, they'll run them alongside the article."

"What?" Jordan's ears perked up at this piece of information. "Oh, Ben!" she said excitedly. "Does this mean you've won your case? Lily's going to be saved after all?"

"Yep," he conceded, a hint of a smile warming his face at last. "The board decided to go along with me. We're moving on it right away."

"That's wonderful!" Pushing back the chair, Jordan rose spontaneously to her feet. "Congratulations!" She took a step toward him. Her impulse was to touch him, to hug him or shake his hand at least. But then she thought better of it and awkwardly wavered where she stood, her fingers resting nervously on the edge of the desk.

Apparently Ben sensed the difficulty in the moment as well. He frowned and stuffed his hands deep into the pockets of his bulky denim jacket. "I think you should be there," he told her gruffly. "You could observe the capture, talk to the photographer, maybe write a brief explanation to go along with the pictures."

"All right," she said.

"Well." He nodded curtly, signaling that the conversation was now officially over. "I'll let you know when it happens."

The call came early Saturday morning. Sometime around dawn, Lily had blundered into the culvert trap that had been set for her, and Ben quickly alerted everyone involved in the undertaking. Jordan tumbled sleepily out of bed and hurried to the designated location.

The transaction unfolded with remarkable ease. Despite her resolve to remain detached and professional, Jordan found herself admiring Ben's every move. Although she ached whenever she looked at him, she had to admit the man really knew what he was doing. She noted the skillful, caring way he handled the bear, sedating her with a syringe attached to a long pole so that she received just the proper dosage, orchestrating everything so that the whole mission was accomplished long before Lily woke up.

"I've looked over that article," Dave Buchanan remarked later as they were all sharing a celebratory beer from an ice chest in the middle of a sunny meadow. "Pretty darn good. You and Ben make quite a team."

"Ah...thanks." Jordan was instantly flustered. "But it was just this one project. We're not actually...a team."

"Well, you should be. I've got lots of work for him. I'm always trying to get him to contribute to the magazine. But he simply will not do it."

"I know. He has a pathological aversion to blank paper."

Dave laughed. "Tell me about it!" he said. "We offered him a book contract last year. We're connected to a publishing house. Did he mention it?"

"I believe my sister said something once. About Ben writing, or not writing, a book."

"The offer's still good. You know, that man—" Dave gestured at Ben with his Heineken bottle "—knows more about bears and a whole bunch of other stuff than anybody else in this country. And he ought to share some of that expertise. I think a book could turn out very nicely."

"Good luck," Jordan told him. "Good luck getting him to sign another contract."

"Ms McKenna—" he held her arm and leaned toward her conspiratorially "—Jordan, why don't you talk to him?"

"I beg your pardon?"

"Convince him to do it. Help him. Just like you did this last time. He can provide the content. You provide the style."

She shook her head. "I'm sorry. I really don't think that would work out very well."

"Sure it would! You guys are a perfect complement for one another. I can tell! I've got a nose for these things." He tapped the side of his.

"Dave—"

"Listen to me! I'm twenty years in this business. I know whereof I speak. Ben Gerard has a ton of experience. He's a great storyteller. But he's a little wild and woolly. He's been out in the woods too long. He needs someone in his life to provide some kind of framework. A bit of discipline. He needs someone to challenge him."

"Maybe so," she conceded. "But I'm afraid it's not going to be me."

"Why not? You've got the brains. You're a smart lady."

"Perhaps, but—"

"And God knows you're pretty. How could a man say no to you?"

"Dave!"

"Okay. Okay." He held up his hands in mock retreat. "I'm not saying you have to marry him. Just write this book. The two of you. Three hundred and fifty pages. Do it for posterity."

"You're a devil, do you know that?"

He laughed again. "Not me," he said. "I just know a natural partnership when I see one."

How could she tell him that the "partnership," or what was left of it, was in shambles? After making a few brief obligatory introductions, Ben had ignored her for most of the afternoon. It was only later when she climbed into her car and was preparing to drive home that he appeared suddenly, knocking on her window.

Jordan rolled it down. "Yes?" Her heart had risen to her throat.

"Your check." Ben reached into the pocket of his jacket and pulled it out. "Fifty per cent of the total amount. Isn't that what we agreed upon?"

"Y-yes. Fine."

Without another word, he deposited it into her shaky hand and then he was gone, a lone dark figure disappearing into the dusk. For a moment Jordan sat there, staring at the scrap of paper. And then she began to cry.

It was really over. Now that the work was complete, they no longer had any reason to see each other. Knowing Ben's propensity for disappearing into the wilderness, she doubted very much whether he'd turn up again at the lodge, at least not while she was there. Jordan leaned forward and rested her head against the steering wheel as the big heavy tears rolled down her cheeks and plopped onto the check, blurring the ink.

TIME PASSED. July turned into August and her supposition proved to be correct. Ben had studiously avoided the inn, and now, according to Pete, he was camping out somewhere in the wilds of King's Can-

yon, monitoring Lily over the radio. At Hallie's insti-
gation, Pete was planning to trek in and spend a
couple of days with him.

"You're running yourself ragged," she'd told her
husband during a recent visit. "You're working all day
at the lodge. You're coming down here every evening
to see me. It's too much. Why don't you take your
sleeping bag and spend a couple of days with Ben at
that campsite? Now please! I want you to stop worrying. I've got Nurse Gibson and besides, this child
isn't going to be here for at least another month."

Finally, albeit reluctantly, Pete agreed to go. Jordan saw him off. Backpack in hand, he stopped by the
desk as she was sorting through the afternoon mail.
"Are you sure you can manage?" he asked for the
thousandth time.

"Absolutely," she said.

"Any messages you want me to deliver to Ben?"

Jordan shook her head.

"Not even a hug and a kiss?" he teased.

"Absolutely not."

Pete cocked his head to one side. "What's the matter? You two seemed pretty cozy last Fourth of July.
Did you have a splat?"

"The word is 'spat.' And it's none of your business, my dear brother-in-law."

"I thought something must've happened." He eyed
her with a mixture of sympathy and curiosity. "You've
been looking kind of sad-eyed, Jordan."

"Oh, bosh. I have not."

"Uh-huh. You're one melancholy baby. And since
you won't tell me what it's about, I guess I'll just have
to ask Ben."

"Don't you dare!" she flared. "Don't you dare!"

"Wow. Must've been pretty serious."

"It was never serious!" she insisted. "It was totally inconsequential. But I want you to keep your mouth shut nonetheless."

"You McKenna women." He shook his head in amusement. "You're both so bossy." Pulling a map from his pocket, he laid it on the desk. "Well, I'm off. If there's any problem, this is where I'll be."

"Thanks, Pete. And have a good time." Holding a couple of letters, Jordan waved him out the door. She really hoped he wouldn't say anything to Ben. She was convinced no good could come of it, and besides, she was having a hard-enough time getting over the man without Pete complicating the issue.

But could she get over him? Jordan tapped the letters pensively against her lips. Would she ever? She had to! She simply had to forget him and get on with the rest of her life.

Glancing at the envelopes, she realized with a start that they were addressed to her. The topmost was from her old boss at Weinstein, O'Connor and Associates. The handwriting on the second was Scott's. Picking up the silver knife on the desk, she slit them open. The business letter read . . .

Dear Ms McKenna,
I thought you were foolish to leave us, but now I think you're foolish if you don't come back. I'm not sure if you've been keeping track, but the campaign you designed for Adonis has been far more successful than any of us could have predicted.

Please give me a call at the office as soon as you receive this letter. I'm prepared to offer you a better position and a substantial raise. I believe you can have a very exciting future with us and I'd be personally happy to have you on the team again.

> All the best,
> Sid Weinstein

Well, well, well, Jordan marveled, Scott had been right in his prediction after all. Mr. Weinstein had not actually driven up into the Sierras in search of her, but he did want her back. Maddening as the whole Adonis campaign had been, she couldn't help but feel complimented. Besides, her shaky self-esteem was in need of a few kind strokes at present. Replacing the note in its envelope, she turned her attention to Scott's letter.

Dear Jordan,
I said I wouldn't push but I can encourage you, can't I? Sweetheart, I hope you're planning to come back to the city in the fall. I hope you've given us some thought!

Seeing you again convinced me. I'm willing to do everything I can to make this relationship work. This time I'm a little older—much wiser, I hope—and I'm waiting to hear from you!

> Scott

"Why would you even consider it?" Hallie exclaimed when Jordan relayed the news to her over the phone. "You left that life behind! Why would you go back to it? What are you running away from, Mary Jordan?"

"I'm not running away from anything," Jordan insisted defensively. "And it's not the same situation! It's a whole new ball game."

"How so?"

"Well..."

"Start with the job first."

"I'd be an executive, for one thing. Part of the reason I was unhappy before was because I didn't have any clout. I was at everybody's mercy. This time I'd have more say-so. I could pick and choose to some extent...."

"Do you really want to be an ad copywriter?"

"I have to do something! I can't stay up here and pick berries and chop wood for the rest of my life!"

"What about Dave Buchanan? He was interested in your work."

"Dave is only interested in me as part of a team. With Ben."

"Ah, Ben!" Hallie echoed. "I knew that name was going to come up! Okay, let's get to the really important part of this conversation."

"Hallie—"

"Have you fallen in love with him?"

"No! I told you—"

Hallie laughed. "You've told me a little, Mary Jordan, but I think you've left out a whole lot. All right, I'll ask the question another way. Are you in love with Scott?"

Jordan hesitated. She should have known better than to call her sister. When Hallie felt strongly about something, she did not hesitate to rake a person over the coals. "He's changed. He really has. He's been going to see this therapist—"

"I know. You told me."

"Everything that used to frustrate me about him before—"

"Is suddenly miraculously different?"

"Maybe. Maybe not. I won't know until I spend some time with him. But he really seems to care for me now. And he wants the same things I do."

"Such as?"

"Marriage. A home. Something ongoing and permanent and real."

"Do you love him?"

"I think maybe I ought to give him another chance."

"Do you love him?" Hallie repeated. "In your heart of hearts? Could you?"

Jordan sighed and shook her head. She knew what the truth was. "No."

"All right then!"

"Oh, Hallie." She crumpled the note. "I feel so mixed up. What am I gonna do?"

"Don't despair. You'll sort through all of this. And you'll find a job. Copywriting, journalism . . . it really doesn't matter as long as it's something you enjoy."

"I know."

"But now I'm back to my original question. I can't help feeling that you're very unhappy about something, Mary Jordan, and you've seized upon these invitations as a possible way out of your misery."

Jordan could sense her throat beginning to close off. All the emotion she'd been trying to ignore for the past several weeks threatened to rise up and overwhelm her. For a moment, she could say nothing.

"Is it Ben?" Hallie asked gently, after a pause.

"Yes," she choked.

"Want to tell me what happened?"

Bit by bit, Jordan poured out the whole story. Her feelings for Ben. His adamantly negative stance on relationships. His discovery of the poems. Her own deception.

"Good grief," Hallie said when she was done.

"I didn't know what else to do." Jordan gulped, brushing away a wayward tear. "He's still in love with Mary. In his eyes, I'm just some second-class diversion."

"Oh, Jordan, I wish I didn't weigh five hundred pounds. I'd come over there and shake some sense into both of you."

"Hallie, it's hardly that simple!"

"Maybe not. But it sounds to me as if each of you is bent on throwing away happiness with both hands."

"I beg your pardon?"

"Ben," her sister began, "is apparently very jealous of a man you're not in love with."

"Hallie—"

"And you, Mary Jordan, are giving up the field to a ghost."

"Mary's still very much alive—in his mind."

"Oh, I don't doubt that he loved her. Maybe he still does and always will. But she doesn't have to be your adversary."

"What do you mean?"

"Oh, for heaven's sake! The human spirit is capable of encompassing all kinds of love."

"But Ben refuses to even—"

"He's scared."

"What?"

"Oh, I know he's a macho guy. He climbs mountains and flies helicopters and talks to bears. But in the most difficult arena of all—the heart—he's a little bit scared. You have to help him."

"How?"

"By being brave yourself. By not giving up. But letting him know how you really feel."

"How did you get to be so wise?"

"All pregnant women are wise," Hallie joked. "We hold the mysteries of the universe within us. Or didn't you know?"

Jordan hugged the telephone. Everything her sister was saying made a great deal of sense, but still something in her was not fully convinced. "He told me he'll never marry, Hallie! I ignored it the first time and then he spelled it out. Wouldn't I be a fool not to listen?"

"Mary Jordan! Look at what's happened. Do you think Ben would be so upset and aloof now if he didn't care about you? He's not exactly taking this in his stride."

"No, but—"

"Then what's stopping you? Cowardice? Your silly pride?"

"Maybe," she moaned. "Oh, I wish I knew what he's thinking! What if you're wrong, Hallie? What if we're both wrong? To go to him and tell him that I love him... What if he feels nothing for me but scorn? It's such a risk!"

"Of course it is! But if you want something badly enough, it's worth taking that risk. It's worth going through hell for. Believe me, I know."

Putting her own dilemma to one side for a moment, Jordan considered her sister's situation. Here was Hallie, inching her way through a difficult pregnancy, risking her own life to bring a child into the world. "You're right," she said at last. "If you can do what you're doing, well, then I'll just have to find a way. When Ben comes back, I'll call him. I promise I will. Hallie?"

The line was strangely silent. For once, her loquacious sister had absolutely nothing to say.

"Hallie? Will you be there for me? Will you patch me up if he says no and I fall to pieces?" Still there was no answer. Jordan wondered if they had been disconnected. She jiggled the cord. "Hallie?"

"Ms McKenna?" The new voice belonged to Nurse Gibson.

"Yes?" she responded, confused.

"I'm afraid your sister isn't doing very well."

"Oh dear! I've upset her. I've talked way too much."

"No, no," the woman assured her, "it wasn't you. This started earlier. Is her husband there?"

"I'm afraid he's gone camping."

"Is there any way you can contact him?"

"I'm not sure. Why?"

Again the line was silent. Anxiously, she waited for some kind of response. "Ms McKenna," the nurse said at last, her voice so serious and so even that it frightened Jordan, "we're going to the hospital. If you can find Mr. Brundin, I suggest you do so."

"Is the baby coming?"

"Possibly. I can't talk now. I have to go." There was a click. Jordan stared at the phone. For a moment she could not bring herself to move.

What to do? Her mind raced. How long had it been since Pete had left? An hour? She'd read the two letters several times and had a cup of tea before she'd decided to call Hallie. No doubt Pete was well on his way by now. Jordan grabbed the map and studied it for a clue.

Judging from the penciled outline, he was taking the road north out of Grant Grove and east into King's Canyon. He'd park his car at the little red X and then he'd start to hike. "I have to catch up with him," Jordan whispered to herself. "I have to find him. Fast!"

Five minutes later, she was on the highway. As luck would have it, the afternoon was sunny and fair and the park was crowded with tourists. To her increasing distress, Jordan found herself impeded by one slow-moving van after another. It was almost impossible to make good time.

"Please, let him stop for gas," she prayed. "Let him stop for supplies. Anything!" She knew that if Pete had already abandoned his vehicle and begun his trek into the wilderness, her job would be twice as hard. "Let him stop for a cup of coffee...."

Although neither she nor Pete had talked very much about it, they both had known that when Hallie's time came, the birth might be tricky and difficult. But her sister had been doing so well lately, they had all optimistically assumed she would carry the baby to term.

Well, it was a month early. If she had, in fact, gone into labor, Hallie would be asking for Pete. Of all the people in the world—including Jordan—he'd be the one she'd most want to see.

Frantically, Jordan continued to look for his old tan Chevy. Once she thought she spotted it, parked outside a market in Grant Grove. But a glance at the license plate told her it was merely a false alarm.

As the sun was sinking low in the western sky, she found his car at last, exactly where the map had indicated it would be. Jordan pulled in next to it, switched off her engine and climbed out. Her brother-in-law was nowhere in sight. She swore under her breath. Apparently, he'd taken his backpack and struck out for the campsite.

Pulling the map from her pocket, she pored over it again. It couldn't be that much farther. She'd have to go after him. After all, Pete was now carrying a sleeping bag and at least twenty pounds of supplies; that ought to slow him down a bit. She was lithe and unencumbered. She could catch up.

Jordan found the trail head and in a short time she was deep within the wilderness. The path was rocky and steeper than she'd expected, and between the exertion and her panic she was soon out of breath. "Calm down," she ordered herself. "Calm down. You'll find him!" Wiping the perspiration from her forehead, forcing herself to take long even breaths, she pushed on.

Twilight deepened gradually into evening. A sliver of a new moon was rising over her shoulder. Jordan felt as if she had been walking forever. "Just a little farther," she promised herself. "Around the next bend. You'll be there soon."

To her right, just ahead, something stirred in the underbrush, a scurrying sound of an animal or a bird, frightening her. Her old fear of the gathering darkness flared up and almost sent her running in the opposite direction, back toward the safety of the car.

"Can't give up now!" She clenched her fists inside the pockets of her jacket. "Can't!" She remembered the night Ben had left her alone in the parking lot in the redwood forest. What was it he had said then? *You can see a little if you concentrate, and the rest is easy....* Repeating his words, Jordan continued up the path. A few minutes later, she ran smack into a low-hanging branch of a tree. As it scraped against her brow, she stumbled and cried out.

The rest is easy if you use your intuition. Regaining her balance, she willed herself forward. Step by step, she ascended the trail, placing her confidence in some power she wasn't sure she possessed. Hallie was at the hospital! She had to find Pete. Jordan called his name. The sound came echoing back to her off the walls of the canyon. She took a deep breath. And then she called for Ben.

PERCHED ON A ROCK at the edge of his campsite, Ben watched as the stars appeared, diamondlike, overhead. He'd left Pete settling his gear inside the tent and come out here to view the spectacle in the night sky.

He'd been camping alone for almost a week and it felt odd having company. Pete seemed bound and determined to tell him all the news. There was a lull at the lodge but a large crowd was expected on the weekend.

Hallie was fine. Pascal had invented a new dessert. Jordan was blue.

Ben flinched and shifted his position. He'd rather not hear about it. If Jordan was sad or happy, if she'd moved back to Los Angeles, if she'd married or gone to hell in a handwagon, it was really none of his business. He didn't want to think about her at all.

But of course that was impossible. The moment he relaxed his guard, she floated into his thoughts, siren-like, a persistent vision. He could almost feel her presence, smell her scent. He could almost hear her voice, a faint music carried on the currents of the southerly breeze.

"Ben . . ."

"Go away," he whispered.

"Ben!"

Something in the sound made his skin prickle and the hair on the back of his neck stand up. Opening his eyes, Ben leaped to his feet and glanced about. Someone was out there. He was sure of it. He scanned the horizon. "Hello," he called. "Over here."

High above him, on the edge of a rocky ledge, a person appeared. A woman. "Ben?" she said.

"Jordan?"

Eagerly she waved her arms. He heard her speak his name, her voice filled with relief. He watched as she began to descend. And then he saw her fall.

CHAPTER TEN

THE NIGHTMARE was happening again. Ben watched it unfold almost in slow motion: the woman high above him on the ledge...her body off balance... arms flailing...pitching headlong...falling...falling. "No!" he shouted as he sprang forward. Then he was running—but not nearly fast enough. There was the sound of rocks tumbling, twigs snapping and the girl slip-sliding down the hillside, powerless to stop.

He caught her in his arms just as she reached the bottom.

"Darling?" he whispered. But she was very still. Her head rested limply against his chest, her hair tangled about her face. Brushing it back with one hand, he cupped her cheek. "Say something!" he begged. "Come on! Talk to me!"

There was no response. The world had ceased to breathe. Ben knelt and cradled her in his lap. "Please," he said. "Please!"

And then, almost imperceptibly, her eyelids fluttered. In a moment she opened them and looked up at him as if she didn't quite know where she was. "Ben?" she murmured.

He held her close. She was all right. Jordan Mc-Kenna. She was safe and secure in his arms. Mary was dead and gone these many years but Jordan was alive. Here and now. In the present. "Yes," he said, burying his mouth in her hair.

Alerted by the noise, Pete had emerged from the tent and was hurrying over to see what had happened. "Jordan?" he said. "What happened? Are you okay?"

"I think so," she ventured in a faint voice. "I'm just...a little shook up. I think I knocked the wind out of myself."

"Well, don't move," Ben advised solicitously. "Wait until you're good and ready."

"I'll get some brandy." Pete headed for the supplies.

Dizzy still, she clung to him. As he stroked her hair, Ben saw the angry bruise on her forehead. "I hope you don't have a concussion," he said, touching the perimeter delicately with his fingertips. "Jordan, what were you thinking of running around in the wilds in the dark?"

"I did what you said," she asserted softly, "and used my intuition, but it must be kind of rusty. I walked into a tree."

"You mad girl. Let's get you inside where you can lie down."

"No, no!" she protested. "We have to go. We have to leave. Now!"

"Why?"

"It's Hallie."

"What about Hallie?" Pete had returned with the flask.

"She's been taken to the hospital. I think the baby..." With an effort, Jordan managed to sit up. "The baby's on its way."

"You're kidding."

She shook her head. "I was talking to her on the phone when it started."

Pete swayed in his tracks. "I knew better than to take this trip!" he declared. "Something was bound to happen the moment I left."

"I'll grab the flashlights," Ben volunteered. "Jordan, do you think you can walk?"

"Yes."

"Are you sure?"

Standing up, she dusted off her hands and knees. "I'm...fine," she said. "Don't worry about me."

The descent through the canyon proved much easier than the journey up. In less than an hour the three had reached the automobiles. Opting to leave Jordan's Fiat where it was, they piled into Pete's Chevy and took off.

Ben drove, and Jordan sat between the two men. From time to time she held Pete's hand. "She'll be all right," she promised, the assurance intended as much for herself as for him.

He nodded.

"The baby's eight months along. And with genes from you and Hallie, he's bound to be a scrapper."

"No matter what happens," Pete said, the tone of his voice quietly acknowledging the gravity of the situation, "it's all been worth it."

"Now Pete—"

"I mean it! The ten years I've spent with Hallie have been the best of my whole life. I wouldn't have missed them for anything."

"There'll be many more."

"God willing," he said. "God willing."

When they reached the hospital, Hallie had been in labor for some time. Dr. Simon was cautious but encouraging. "We're prepared to take emergency measures of course, but so far she's holding her own. Keep your fingers crossed."

Once again, in the wee hours of the morning, Ben and Jordan found themselves in the lounge, drinking coffee and waiting for news. Pete had been allowed to remain with Hallie.

"It doesn't stop, does it?" Ben commented. He sat on the edge of a sofa, his elbows resting on his knees.

"What do you mean?" she asked. "What doesn't stop?"

"Life!" He gestured at the walls around him. "People dying, people getting born. The relentless flow of it. It just...never...stops."

Jordan shook her head. "I guess not," she said softly, realizing for the first time how difficult it must be for him to spend time inside a hospital. How many memories the place must evoke!

"You know, Jordan, for a long time I've tried to stay aloof. I thought as long as I kept to myself and didn't get too mixed up in other people's lives, I could spare myself some of the grief."

"You're thinking of Mary?" she said.

He nodded. "When I lost her, I swore that was it for me. It was a wonderful relationship but the price was just too great."

"It's a terrible price," she agreed.

"I mourned her for years. And meanwhile I built this...wall around myself." He was silent for a moment, then continued. "I had friends, of course. I had relationships with women. But I made certain that nobody got too close."

"I know."

"Dumb, huh?" His laugh was full of rue.

"Understandable."

Ben stood and paced restlessly to the window. "Well, tonight it all came home to me. Jordan, when I saw you take that fall down that hillside..."

She pressed her hand against her chest. "I was careless and...oh, Ben, it must've looked like the same accident happening all over again."

"Exactly. And it made me realize how much...how much you mean to me!"

"How much I...?"

"And this wall, this stupid wall I'd worked so hard to maintain, it cracked open. I can't dam up what's inside and I guess I was crazy to try in the first place!"

Jordan stared at him, too amazed to speak.

"Then, later in the car, when Pete talked about Hallie, about all the years they've spent together, I thought to myself, 'Ben, you fool! You're letting so much valuable time go by. You're wasting it. Here beside you sits this lovely, wonderful woman, and you were almost ready to let her walk out of your life.'"

Rising, she went over to him.

"I love you," he said. "I do. Maybe it's a little late for me to be telling you..."

She slipped her arms around his neck. "No," she whispered. "Never too late...." Her voice was thick with tears.

Ben crushed her to him. She drank in the sweet cedary smell of him as she buried her face and wept into the lapel of his jacket. "Don't cry," he said.

"I'm not unhappy," she claimed between hiccups. "Ben, I love you so much, I—"

He found her lips then, his kiss both tender and urgent. Jordan laced her fingers through his thick dark hair, cradling his head in her hands. For a time the rest of the world disappeared. The hospital, the lights, the waiting room, all vanished into one white blur. "Love you," she breathed. "Only you...."

"What's your fiancé going to say?" he murmured huskily in her ear.

"I don't have a fiancé."

"Jordan! Those poems...?"

"They were all about you."

"But you insisted they weren't, so I thought—"

"No! Every single one of them was about you. I was ashamed to tell you."

"But I really thought—"

"—they were about Scott. I know. You jumped to that conclusion and I let you. I was afraid... Oh Ben, I'm sorry!"

He took her by the shoulders and shook her passionately, affectionately. "Jordan McKenna! Do you have any idea how jealous I was?"

"Were you?" she said with a small smile. "Tell me!"

"You minx! You let me suffer!"

"Not on purpose. I was upset. I thought I meant nothing whatsoever to you."

Ben cupped her face in the palm of his hand. "I was probably in love with you all along," he told her, "but I absolutely would not admit it. I fought it tooth and nail."

"We've both been pretty dumb, haven't we?"

"Crazy."

"Foolish."

"Jordan?" He folded her hands together and pressed them between his own. "Before anything else happens, before I let you out of my sight, there's something I have to ask...."

She gazed at him wonderingly.

But before he could continue, Pete burst noisily into the room. "Where the hell have you two been?" he shouted. "Do you want to hear the good news or what?"

Jordan caught her breath.

"I'm a father!" He ran over, picked Jordan up and spun her around the lounge. "You're an aunt! Hallie just had a baby boy!"

"Oh, Pete!" she squealed, hugging him back. "That's fabulous! Is she . . . is everything all right?"

"Your sister came through like a trooper. She had a natural delivery. Dr. Simon couldn't believe it! None of the complications arose. She's fine!"

"And the baby?"

"Six pounds. A little fellow but he's perfect. He's just beautiful! I'm crazy about him!" Pete laughed. He released her and turned to embrace Ben. "Petter McKenna Brundin!" he announced. "We're going to call him Mac."

"Congratulations!" Ben pounded him on the back. "When do we get to meet this cub of yours?"

"Well, Dr. Simon says if you hurry you can come up right now." He took each of them jubilantly by the arm. "Let's go. Hallie's probably going to conk out pretty soon."

Propped up against large white pillows, Hallie looked both radiant and exhausted. The baby was nestled in the crook of her arm. "He's so sweet," she told Jordan. "He doesn't look at all like a gnome, does he?"

"Not a bit."

"Newborn babies sometimes do, you know."

"He's lovely, Hallie."

"He's got ten little fingers and ten little toes. I counted."

"You did a great job." Jordan leaned over and kissed her sister on the cheek.

"Mary Jordan, sweetheart, Pete told me how you trekked all the way out into King's Canyon to find him. Thank you. It made a big difference having him here."

"Good. I'm glad."

"Ben—" Hallie shifted her gaze to include him "—may I ask you a favor?"

"Yes, ma'am." Stepping forward, he took her hand in his.

"Look after my sister," she bossed.

"Yes, ma'am. I intend to."

"Drive her home and see that she gets some rest. She's had quite a day."

"Yes, ma'am," he repeated with a twinkle in his eye. "Anything else?"

Fatigued as she was, Hallie caught the twinkle. She looked first at Jordan, her eyes narrowing shrewdly, and then again at Ben. "No," she said lightly. "Anything else I leave entirely up to you."

THE SKY WAS JUST BEGINNING to glow with pre-dawn light as they drove up the winding road into the mountains. Jordan sat with her feet curled under her on the front seat of the Chevy. Stretching her arm along the backrest, she gently cupped the nape of Ben's neck. His skin was warm and velvety. "Ask me," she said.

"Hmm?" He gave her an affectionate sidelong glance.

"In the hospital, before Pete rushed in, you were about to ask me something."

"Right." He smiled. "I was."

"Well?"

"Jordan..." Keeping one hand on the wheel, he rested the other on her knee. "I'm not a city person. I hate the smog. I hate the traffic. I hate the whole congested mess. I need elbow room. I was born in the wilderness and I intend to die here."

"I figured as much." She nodded.

"So what about you? You're a..."

"Hothouse flower?"

Ben shook his head. "A rather sophisticated lady. A woman with a career. I know you like those bright lights! Those fancy restaurants..."

"It's true," she said. "I do." Trying to contain her excitement, Jordan gazed past him out the window of the car. "As a matter of fact, Weinstein and O'Connor just offered me a whole new contract. They want me to move back.''

"They do?'' He grimaced.

"Uh-huh.''

"This is a dilemma!'' There was humor in his voice but she could also hear a very real concern. "I can tell you right now I'm not going to live there! And I love you too much to carry on some long-distance affair.''

"What did you have in mind?'' she asked. "Tell me how you see it.''

"Okay. First of all you turn down the offer. You live up here with me. I have a wonderful house. I make more money than I know what to do with...''

"Are you proposing to keep me?'' She tangled her fingers into his hair and gave it a pull.

"Ouch!'' He grinned.

"Am I to be a kept woman?''

"I'm proposing! Period! I'm asking you to marry me, damn it!''

"You are?'' Jordan could feel her insides turning to jelly.

"Yes!'' With a sharp twist of the wheel, Ben pulled the car into a turnout. In the distance before them, the magnificent countryside was turning a soft peachy pink. "Yes! What do you want me to do, you minx! Get down on my knees?''

"Would you?'' she asked, misty-eyed.

Yanking the door open, Ben climbed out and pulled her after him. In a moment he had seated her upon a rock and knelt before her. "Jordan McKenna,'' he said. "Marry me! Please!''

She looked at him, taking in his beautiful dark eyes, the strength in his hands and shoulders. Behind his head the sun was breaking over the top of a mountain, encircling him in a ring of light. "Yes," she said. And promptly she burst into tears.

"Good grief!" Ben gathered her into his arms. "You are such a crybaby." He kissed the corners of her eyes. "What am I gonna do with you? Huh?"

Reaching inside the fleecy lining of his jacket, Jordan nestled against him. "Hold me," she said.

Ben was glad to oblige.

"Closer!"

"How's this?"

"Perfect," she whispered. "Oh, Ben, do you really mean it?"

"Hey. I'm not letting you get away."

"I was never going to accept that dumb old job. I wasn't!" she confessed. "I just didn't want you to take me too much for granted. I'd...I'd give up all the restaurants and theaters and...hoopla in the world to be with you."

"Good. I'm mighty relieved to hear it."

"You're going to have to teach me a lot of stuff, you know."

"How to bait a hook..."

"How to see in the dark..."

"How to cook a rattlesnake..."

"Yuck!" She shook her head. "I'll love and honor you forever and ever, amen. But there are some things I will not obey."

"All right." He laughed. "Since you're being such a sport, I'll tell you what..."

"What?"

"Every so often, I'll drive you down to Los Angeles, or up to San Francisco."

"Yes?" Jordan was impressed.

"Sure. I'm a liberated fellow. I know how to compromise."

"And . . . ?"

"We'll dine on sushi."

She giggled helplessly.

"We'll take in a show or go to a museum."

"Ben!"

"And then we'll amble over to Beverly Hills. I'm assuming that's where you got that lace whatchamacallit."

"Which?"

He traced the outline on her body.

"Peignoir?"

Ben nodded. "I think you're going to need a few dozen more."

"I think I am," Jordan agreed, kissing him. "And you know what? I'm going to need a new typewriter, as well."

"For what purpose, my darlin'?"

"According to Dave Buchanan, you and I are natural partners. We're supposed to be writing a book."

"Oh gosh," he groaned. "That bloody book!"

"You're to provide the content. I'll supply the style. We'll do it for posterity."

"What posterity?" Ben was resistant. "Whose posterity?"

"Well," she said, "there's Mac Brundin, to begin with."

Ben thought for a moment. "He's only a couple of hours old, but okay, I guess he does count as posterity."

"And then...someday perhaps...yours and mine."

"True," he said huskily. "How soon, ah, do you think we ought to start?"

"On the book?"

He nosed his way into her hair and covered her ear with his mouth. "On the posterity, so to speak."

Jordan smiled. "Oh ... someday..."

"Someday soon?"

"Very soon," she promised.

He kissed her temple and then he found her mouth. "Sooner!"

"Soonest."

"That's way too long."

"Ben..."

"Come on, lady." Rising, he took her hand. His eyes were soft with feeling. "I'm taking you home."

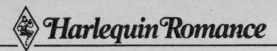
Harlequin Romance

Coming Next Month

2833 SOFTLY FLITS A SHADOW Elizabeth Duke
Jilted! A broken-hearted American embarks on her honeymoon
cruise alone and attracts the attention of a fellow passenger,
who assumes she's out to catch a husband. After what she's
been through?

2834 TEMPEST IN THE TROPICS Roumelia Lane
The same meddling forestry man who's threatening her
father's Guyanese timber plantation tries to stand in the way of
a fiery daughter's plan to marry the one man she thinks could
ensure her father's future.

2835 LOVE BY DEGREE Debbie Macomber
To make ends meet when she returns to university, a mature
student plays housemother to three lovable Washington college
boys. But instead of encouragement she gets the third degree
from the owner of their cozy home.

2836 THE NIGHT IS DARK Joanna Mansell
Never get emotionally involved with clients—it's the number
one rule for Haversham girls. But an assignment in East Africa
with wildlife adventure writer Kyle Allander proved that love
makes its own rules!

2837 THE APOLLO MAN Jean S. MacLeod
Still bitter over her childhood sweetheart's sudden departure
from the Isle of Cyprus six years ago, a young islander is
suspicious of his reasons for returning . . . wary of her memories
of love.

2838 THE HARLEQUIN HERO Dixie McKeone
A romance novel fan adopts her favorite heroin's sophisticated
image to attract a living breathing hero. But her plan backfires
when he takes a page from the same book to woo the woman of
his dreams—another woman!

Available in May wherever paperback books are sold, or
through Harlequin Reader Service.

In the U.S.
901 Fuhrmann Blvd.
P.O. Box 1397
Buffalo, N.Y. 14240-1397

In Canada
P.O. Box 603
Fort Erie, Ontario
L2A 5X3

ATTRACTIVE, SPACE SAVING BOOK RACK

Display your most prized novels on this handsome and sturdy book rack. The hand-rubbed walnut finish will blend into your library decor with quiet elegance, providing a practical organizer for your favorite hard-or soft-covered books.

Only $9.95

Approximately 16″ x 8″ when assembled

Assembles in seconds!

To order, rush your name, address and zip code, along with a check or money order for $10.70* ($9.95 plus 75¢ postage and handling) payable to *Harlequin Reader Service*:

> Harlequin Reader Service
> Book Rack Offer
> 901 Fuhrmann Blvd.
> P.O. Box 1325
> Buffalo, NY 14269-1325
>
> *Offer not available in Canada.*

*New York residents add appropriate sales tax.

BKR-1R

New This spring
Harlequin Category Romance Specials!
New Mix

4 Regencies—for more wit, tradition, etiquette...and romance

2 Gothics—for more suspense, drama, adventure...and romance

Regencies

A Hint of Scandal by Alberta Sinclair
She was forced to accept his offer of marriage, but could she live with her decision?

The Primrose Path by Jean Reece
She was determined to ruin his reputation and came close to destroying her own!

Dame Fortune's Fancy by Phyllis Taylor Pianka
She knew her dream of love could not survive the barrier of his family tradition....

The Winter Picnic by Dixie McKeone
All the signs indicated they were a mismatched couple, yet she could not ignore her heart's request....

Gothics

Mirage on the Amazon by Mary Kistler
Her sense of foreboding did not prepare her for what lay in waiting at journey's end....

Island of Mystery by Margaret M. Scariano
It was the perfect summer job, or so she thought—until it became a nightmare of danger and intrigue.

Don't miss any of them!